D0043494

THE OBEDIENT DEMON

It was several days since my master, the wizard Maldivius, had left and his apprentice, Grax, had sneaked away during his absence. But I remembered his orders well.

"You are not indentured to think, but to follow orders," he had demanded. "The first person to enter my sanctum before my return is to be eaten alive! No exceptions."

Now, as I was refilling the water clock, I heard boot heels in the maze. Presently, the young apprentice stood in the entrance—the first person to enter the sanctum.

"Hola there, stupid!" Grax cried. "Poor old demon Zdim! Can you do naught but sit there and look ugly?"

He had time for one short scream before I sprang upon the lad, tore him to pieces, and ate him.

I was comforted to think I was but obeying orders.

Also by L. Sprague de Camp
Published by Ballantine Books:

ANCIENT ENGINEERS

THE TRITONIAN RING

LEST DARKNESS FALL

LOVECRAFT: A BIOGRAPHY

THE BEST OF L. SPRAGUE DE CAMP

THE COMPLEAT ENCHANTER *(with Fletcher Pratt)*

THE
FALLIBLE
FIEND

L. Sprague de Camp

'A Del Rey Book'

BALLANTINE BOOKS • NEW YORK

A Del Rey Book
Published by Ballantine Books

Copyright © 1972, 1973 by Ultimate Publishing Co., Inc.;
Copyright © 1973 by L. Sprague de Camp.

All rights reserved. Published in the United States by Ballantine
Books, a division of Random House, Inc., New York, and simul-
taneously in Canada by Random House of Canada, Limited,
Toronto, Canada.

ISBN 0-345-29367-3

Manufactured in the United States of America

First Ballantine Books Edition: May 1981

Cover art by Bill Schmidt

To Isaac Asimov,
who started after I did but
has natheless written more books.

Ego te olim assequar!

CONTENTS

I

DOCTOR MALDIVIUS

On the first day of the Month of the Crow, in the fifth year of King Tonio of Xylar (according to the Novarian calendar) I learnt that I had been drafted for a year's service on the Prime Plane, as those who dwell there vaingloriously call it. They refer to our plane as the Twelfth, whereas from our point of view, ours is the Prime Plane and theirs, the twelfth. But, since this is the tale of my servitude on the plane whereof Novaria forms a part, I will employ their terms.

I at once repaired to the court of the Provost of Ning. I had known the Provost before his elevation. In fact, as boy-demons we had hunted flitflowers together in the Marshes of Kshak, and I hoped to claim exemption on the basis of this old friendship. I said:

"My dear old Hwor, how good to see you again! All goes well with you, I trust?"

"Zdim Akh's son," said Hwor sternly, "you should know better than to address your Provost, in the discharge of his office, in familiar terms. Let us have due decorum."

"Well—ah—" I stammered. "I beg your pardon, Lord Provost. Now, about this notice of induction, I believe I may claim deferment."

"On what grounds?" said the Provost in his most grating official voice.

"Imprimis, on the ground that my mate, Yeth Ptyg's daughter, has just laid a clutch of eggs and needs me at home to help guard them. Secundus, having been trained in philosophy and logic, I am unsuited to the kind of rough-and-tumble, adventuresome life, which, I am told, awaits one on the Prime Plane. Tertius, the philosopher Khrum, whose apprentice I am, has de-

1

parted on a fortnight's fishing trip, leaving his effects, correspondence, and pupils in my care. And quartus, our crop of rabbages is nearly ripe and will need me to harvest it."

"Deferment denied. Imprimis, I shall send a bailiff to help your mate in guarding the eggs and collecting the crop. Secundus, besides your philosophy, you are also well-read in Prime Plane history and biography and so are better fitted to cope with the exigencies of that world than most demons sent thither. Tertius, a few days off will not harm the respected Khrum's pupils and correspondents. And quartus, we must have somebody, and your name has come up in the drawing. Our growing population and rising standard of living require more and more iron, and private interests must yield to the common good. So you shall report here three days hence for evocation."

Three days later, I bit Yeth good-bye and returned to the Provost's court. Hwor gave me parting advice:

"You will find the average Prime Planer a soft, weak being. Unarmed, he presents no threat. The folk of that plane, however, have conceived an array of lethal weapons, wherewith they practice the barbaric art of war. Do not needlessly expose yourself to harm from such weapons. Whereas we demons are stronger, tougher, and longer-lived than the men of the Prime Plane, it is not yet known for sure whether we have souls, which upon death move on to another dimension, as do the souls of Prime Planers."

"I will be careful," I said. "Khrum tells me that the Prime Plane afterworld is an extraordinary place, where gods are feeble wraiths, magic is virtually impotent, and most of the work is done by machinery. He assures me that, to preserve the symmetry of the cosmos, there should logically be an afterworld related to our plane in the same way—"

"I daresay," said Hwor. "You must excuse me, but I have a busy schedule. Take care for your safety, render faithful service, and obey the laws of the Prime Plane."

"But how if these laws be mutually contradictory? Or if my master command me to commit an illegality?"

"You will have to work that out as best you can."
He pointed a claw. "Kindly stand on yonder pentacle."

I stepped to the center of the diagram, and the technician closed the figure with a piece of charcoal. Then I had to wait half an hour by the time candle.

At last the lines of the pentacle glowed red. Thereby I knew that he who had contracted for me had uttered his incantation. And then—*fthoomp!*—the Provost's courtroom vanished and I stood, instead, in a rough-hewn underground chamber, on a pentacle just like that in my own world. I knew that a hundred-pound ingot of iron had rested upon the pentacle whereon I now stood, and that this ingot had taken my place in the Twelfth Plane. Our accursed lack of iron compels us to indenture our citizens as bondservants to the Prime Planers.

The chamber was circular, about twenty feet in diameter and half as high. The surrounding wall had a single opening into a dark tunnel. The air had a dank, dead quality.

A pair of ornate brass lamps illumined the chamber. Volumes crowded bookshelves around the walls. Furnishings included chairs, tables, and a divan, all worn and battered. The tables were littered with bowls, braziers, balances, mortars, and other tools of a wizard's trade. On a small stand rested a holder, in which lay a blue sphere the size of a human being's fist. It was evidently a magical gemstone, for it glowed with a flickering light.

There were two human beings in the chamber. The elder was a thin, stoop-shouldered man almost as tall as I, which is quite tall for a Prime Planer. He had bushy gray whiskers, hair, and eyebrows, and was clad in a patched black robe.

The other was a short, stout, swarthy, black-haired boy of about fifteen years, wearing waistcoat and hose and holding some of the wizard's paraphernalia. My tendrils picked up hostile vibrations from the boy, although at that time I had not known enough Prime Planers to interpret his emotions. From the way the youth shrank from me, however, I inferred that fear comprised a goodly part of them.

"Who are you?" said the elderly one in Novarian.

"I—Zdim Akh's son," I replied slowly. Although I had studied the language in school, I had never conversed with native Novarians. Fluency therefore came to me slowly. "Who—you?"

"I hight Doctor Maldivius, a diviner," replied the man. "This is Grax of Chemnis, my apprentice." He indicated the boy.

"Catfish!" said Grax.

"Mind your manners!" said Maldivius. "The fact that Zdim is indentured gives you no right to bully him."

"What—is—catfish?" I asked.

"A fish found in—ah—rivers and lakes on this plane," explained Maldivius. "That pair of tendrils on your upper lip remind him of the barbels of such a fish. Now, you have contracted to serve me for a year. Is this well understood?"

"Aye."

"Aye, sir!"

I wriggled my tendrils in annoyancē, but this fellow had the upper hand of me. Although I could have broken him in two, my misbehavior would have caused me trouble when I got back to my own plane. Besides, we are told, before submitting to evocation, not to be surprised at anything Prime Planers do.

"Aye, sir," I said.

To one who has never seen a Prime Planer, they are repulsive. Instead of a coat of beautiful blue-gray scales, glistening with a metallic luster, they have soft, almost naked skins in various shades of pink, yellow, and brown. Once denizens of the tropics, they adapt themselves to cooler climes by covering these skins with woven fabrics. Their internal heat, combined with the insulation afforded by these structures, called "garments," enables them to survive cold that would freeze a demon stiff.

Their eyes have round pupils with only a small accommodation to light; hence they are almost blind at night. They have funny little round ears. Their faces are sunken in, their muzzles and fangs being hardly more than vestiges. They have no tails, and their fingers and toes end in flat, rudimentary claws called "nails."

On the other hand, if in appearance and behavior they often seem bizarre, they are extremely clever and ingenious. They are endlessly fertile in thinking up plausible reasons for doing what they wish to do. I was astonished to learn that they have terms like "fiendishly clever" and "devilishly shrewd." Now, "fiend" and "devil" are opprobrious terms, which they apply to us demons—as if we had more of this perverted ingenuity than they!

"Where—am—I?" I asked Maldivius.

"In an underground labyrinth beneath the ruined temple of Psaan, near the town of Chemnis."

"Where is that?"

"Chemnis is in the Republic of Ir, one of the Twelve Nations of Novaria. Chemnis lies at the mouth of our main river, the Kyamos. The city of Ir is nine leagues up the Kyamos. I have repaired this maze and turned the central chamber into my sanctum."

"What would you of me?"

"Your main duty will be to guard this chamber when I am absent. My books and magical accessories—especially that thing—are valuable."

"What is it, sir?"

"Ahem. It is the Sibylline Sapphire, a divinatory crystal of the highest quality. You shall guard it with care, and woe betide you if you carelessly knock over the stand and break the gem!"

"Should I not, then, remove it to one side, where it will not be in way?" I said.

The boy Grax puckered up his face—these human beings have very mobile, expressive faces when one learns to interpret them—in a glare of hostility. "Let me," he said. "I don't trust old Catfish." He moved the stand and turned to me. "Next thing, Master Catfish, you shall cook and clean for us, ha ha!"

"Me, cook and clean?" I said. "That female work! You should have evoked a demoness!"

"Ha!" sneered the youth. "I've been cooking and

cleaning for three years, and I'll warrant it won't hurt you for a change."

I turned to Maldivius, who after all was my master. But the wizard only said: "Grax is correct. As his knowledge of the arcane arts advances, I shall require more and more of his time to assist me. Therefore he cannot continue his domestic duties."

"Well," I said, "I shall endeavor to give satisfaction. But you tell me, sir, that this place is near a town. Why not hire a woman from this town for these tasks? If it be like towns on my plane, there would be unattached females—"

"No argument, O demon! You must follow my orders, literally and exactly, without questioning. I will, however, answer your question. In the first place, the townsfolk would be terrified of you."

"Of me? But, sir, at home I am deemed the mildest and meekest of demons, a quiet student of philosophy—"

"And, second, I should have to teach the wench how to get in and out of this maze. For obvious reasons, I do not wish to publish this information to the world at large. Ahem. Now, to begin your duties, your first task will be to prepare tonight's dinner."

"Gods of Ning! How shall I do that, sir? Must I sally forth to run down and slay some wild creature?"

"Nay, any, my good Zdim. Grax will show you to the kitchen and instruct you. If you begin now, you should have a savory repast ready by sunset."

"But, sir! I can broil a wild fluttersnake over a campfire on a hunting trip, but I have never cooked a real dinner in my life."

"Then learn, servant," said Maldivius.

"Come along, you!" said Grax, who had been lighting a small lanthorn at one of the brass lamps. He led me out of the chamber and into the tunnel. The path bent and wound this way and that, passing a number of branches and forks.

"How on earth do you ever find your way?" I asked.

"How on earff do I effer ffind my vay?" he said, mocking my accent. "You memorize a formula. Going out, 'tis right-left-right-left-left-right-right. Coming in, it's the opposite: left-left-right-right-left-right-left. Canst do that?"

I muttered the formulae. Then I asked: "Why does Doctor Maldivius locate his kitchen so far from his sanctum? The food will be cold by the time the cook gets it to his board."

"Silly! If we cooked inside the maze, the place would be filled with smoke and fumes. You will just have to run with your tray. Here we are."

We had reached the entrance to the maze, where the tortuous corridor straightened out. Doors opened into chambers on either hand, and at the far end I could see daylight.

There were four of these chambers. Two were fitted up as bedrooms; the third was used for storage of the dwellers' possessions. The fourth, next to the exit, was the kitchen. This last had a window cut in one wall.

In the window was mounted a casement with an iron frame and many small, leaded panes. The casement was now open, affording a view. The chamber was built into the side of a cliff, with the waves of the Western Ocean striking rocks at the base of the cliff a score of fathoms below. The cliff curved, so that from the window one had a good view of its precipitous slope. It was raining outside.

A stream of water had been diverted through an earthen pipe into the kitchen, so that it trickled from above into one of a pair of wooden sinks. Grax made a fire on the hearth and set out the spits, cauldrons, frying pans, forks, and other implements of cookery. Then he opened bins containing edibles and explained the nature of each, betimes berating me for my clumsiness and stupidity.

I learnt to interpret his vibrations as manifestations of hatred. I found this hard to understand, since I had done nothing to earn Grax's enmity. I suppose he was jealous of anyone who infringed his monopoly of old Maldivius' time and regard—despite the fact that I was here against my will, earning a meager hundredweight of iron for the use of my people. I envied those who could afford to use iron for mere window casements.

Well, I went through many ordeals during my servitude on the Prime Plane, but never did I experience more exasperation than in preparing that dinner. Grax rattled off his instructions, set the sand glass going to time my cookery, and left me. I tried to follow his directions, but I kept confusing his figures for time, distance from the flame, and so forth.

When I thought I had everything under control, I set out for the sanctum to ask further instructions. I promptly took a wrong turning and got lost in the maze. At last I found myself back at the entrance. With effort, I remembered the formula for entering the labyrinth and this time attained the sanctum without a mistake.

"Where is our dinner?" said Maldivius, sitting with Grax in two of the battered chairs. The twain were drinking, out of pottery cups, the liquor called *olikau*, imported from Paalua across the Western Ocean.

"I must ask you, sir——" and I requested more details. When the magician had given them, I found my way back to the entrance. The kitchen was full of smoke and stench; for, during my absence, the sliced ham, the main item, had burnt to a large black cinder.

I trailed back to the sanctum. "Well," snarled Maldivius, "where is our dinner now?"

I told what had befallen.

"You idiot!" screamed the wizard. "By Zevatas' beard, of all the stupid, blundering, incompetent, feckless fiends I ever did know, you are the worst!"

He snatched up his wand and chased me around the chamber, whacking me on the head and shoulders. An ordinary stick of that size I should hardly have felt, but the wand gives a horrid tingling, burning sensation when it hits. By the third lap around, I began to feel resentment. I could easily have torn Doctor Maldivius limb from limb, but I was kept from doing so by the terms of my indenture and fear of my own government.

"Why don't we trade old Catfish in, boss?" said Master Grax. "Send him back to the Twelfth Plane and demand another one with at least the brains of a hoptoad."

Doctor Maldivius stood panting and leaning on his

wand. "Take this wretched imitation of a demon back to the kitchen and start over."

Grax led me back through the maze, grinning and uttering many a quip on my want of intellect. (It is common practice among human beings to make these meaningless remarks they call "jokes," whereupon they bare their teeth and go "Ha ha ha." This seems to give them pleasure.) When we arrived, I found that all the water in the pot containing the turnips had boiled away, so that the turnips were half burnt and stuck to the pot.

It was three hours after my first arrival in the kitchen before I assembled a passable dinner for this pair of cantankerous conjurors. Then I got lost in the maze again on my way to the sanctum. By the time I found my customers, the victuals were cold. Luckily for me, the twain had by this time drunk so much olikau that they never noticed. Grax was in a fit of giggling. When I asked Maldivius when and what I myself was to eat, he only goggled at me and mumbled: "Huh? What? Who?"

So back I went to the kitchen and cooked my own dinner. It was no gourmet meal, but being ravenous I found it better than anything I have tasted before or since.

During the following days, my cookery improved, albeit I do not think I could ever apply for a post as chef in the palace of a great lord of the Prime Plane. Then, when Grax was out on an errand, Maldivius called me in to the sanctum.

"I am taking the mule to Ir on the morrow," he said. "I hope to be back two or three days thereafter. You will be alone most of the time. I would that you remained here in the sanctum on guard, save for the most necessary occasions. Fetch your repasts in here to eat. You can sleep on the divan."

"Will not Master Grax be here to keep me company, sir?"

"I know not what you mean by 'keeping company,' for it has not escaped me that the feelings betwixt you two can hardly be described as love. In any case, I know from experience that, even if I command Grax to remain, he will sneak off to Chemnis the minute I am out of sight. This is one reason for my having contracted for your services."

"Wherefore does he that, sir?"

Maldivius: "He has a girl in town, whom he visits for purposes of—ah—fornication. I have told him and told him that, to rise into the upper ranks of the profession, one must relinquish such fleshly pleasures. But he pays me no heed. Like most youths, he thinks that everybody older than himself is far gone in senile decay."

"Were you, sir, as abstemious as you wish him to be when you were his age?"

"Shut up and mind your business, you impudent rascal. Ahem. Attend closely. You shall remain on guard here warding my property, especially the Sibylline Sapphire. If anyone enter the sanctum ere I return, you shall devour him instanter."

"Really, sir? I should think—"

"You are not indentured to think, but to follow orders! Listen, comprehend, and obey! The first person to enter the sanctum before my return is to be eaten alive! No exceptions! It is not as if they will not have been warned. Grax has lettered a sign, BEWARE OF THE DEMON, and posted it at the entrance. Do you understand?"

I sighed. "Aye, sir. May I take the liberty of asking the nature of your errand?"

Maldivius chuckled. "It is my chance to make what the vulgar call a 'killing.' For, in my Sapphire, I have seen doom approaching Ir. Since only I am cognizant of this, I should be able to squeeze a respectable fee out of the skinflint Syndics in return for this news."

"Sir, as a citizen of Ir, I should think you would deem it your duty to warn the state regardless of reward—"

"You dare to tell me my duty, sirrah?" Maldivius snatched up his wand as if to strike me but then mastered himself. "Some day I will explain. Suffice it to say that I have no particular loyalty to a city whose judges have fleeced me, whose rich have scorned me, where

my colleagues have plotted against me, and where even
the boys have followed me, throwing stones and hoot-
ing. An I obeyed my urges, I would let their doom
overtake them. But to abandon an opportunity for
profit for a petty revenge were youthful folly. Forget
not your orders, now!"

II

JIMMON THE SYNDIC

I FOLLOWED the wizard up the cliffside stairs to the
top. Around us lay the ruined temple of Psaan, the Novarian god of the sea. The stumps of marble columns
rose in ranks like a company of soldiers magically
turned to stone, while separate column drums and frag-
ments littered the cracked and tilted marble pave.
Grass grew in the cracks. So did shrubs and even a few
trees, which had canted the flags in their growth. There
had once, Maldivius told me, been much more to the
ruins, but for centuries the Chemnites had used the site
as a quarry.

While I saddled up the mule and strapped the doctor's traveling bag to the cantle, Maldivius repeated his
instructions. Then off he went.

Doctor Maldivius was right about his apprentice.
The diviner was hardly out of sight, and I had started
down the stair, when I had to halt to allow Master
Grax, wearing his good doublet and boots, to ascend.
The youth grinned.

"Well, old Catfish," he said, "I'm off to town. I'll
warrant you wish you had what I'm going for!" He
jerked his pelvis to illustrate.

"I own I shall miss my wife," I said, "but—"

"You mean demons have wives, just like people?"

"Of course. What thought you?"

"Methought that when you were fain to increase,

you split down the middle and each half became a whole new demon, as Maldivius says some little water creatures do. Do you futter your wives as we do?"

"Aye, though not the year round, as you Prime Planers seem to."

Grax: "Well, why not come to Chemnis with me? I know a dame—"

"My orders forbid. Besides, I misdoubt that a human woman would enjoy carnal congress with me."

"Why not? Wrong size?"

"Nay; it is the spiny barbs on my male member."

"You actually *have* one?"

"Certes, inside."

"How do your women—demonesses, I suppose I should call them—take the spiny barbs?"

"They find them pleasantly stimulating. But now I needs must take up my post in the central chamber."

"Well, stupid, don't fall asleep and let some thief clean the place out! A couple of boys down in Chemnis wouldn't mind eking out their earnings by a bit of burglary. Expect me back on the morrow."

He strode off on the dusty track that Maldivius had taken. I returned to the sanctum. For several days I had been too busy to digest the food I had eaten and hence had become somewhat bloated. I welcomed the chance to sink into digestive torpor. This lasted into the following day, as I could tell from the little water clock on one of Maldivius' tables.

I had roused myself and was refilling the reservoir of the water clock, when I heard the sound of boot heels in the maze. It might, I thought, be Grax; or it might be an intruder.

Then I remembered how insistent Doctor Maldivius had been about my devouring the first person to enter the sanctum before his return. No exceptions, he had said; I must follow his orders literally and implicitly. When I tried to ask whether he was fain to except Master Grax, he had shut me off. Meseemed he wished me, for some arcane reason, to treat Grax as I would any other intruder.

Presently, Grax stood in the entrance with a sack of edibles, bought in the village, on one shoulder. "Hola there, stupid!" he cried. "Poor old Catfish, can do nought better than sit in the sanctum and look ugly, like the idol of some heathen god—ho, what do you?"

Grax had advanced into the sanctum as he spoke. He had time for but one short scream as I sprang upon the youth, tore him to pieces, and ate him. I must say that he was pleasanter as provender than as a living companion.

Some things, however, perturbed me. For one, the brief struggle had disordered the room. A table was overset, and gore was spattered far and wide. Fearing that Maldivius would chastise me for sloppy housekeeping, I set to work with bucket, mop, and broom and in an hour had almost erased all traces of the fracas. The larger bones of the late Grax I stacked neatly on an empty bookshelf. A gout of blood had struck a copy of *Material and Spiritual Perfection in Ten Easy Lessons,* by Voltiper of Kortoli, on the bookshelves. The blood had run between the pages, staining several with a large red blot.

As I worked, another thought oppressed me. On the Twelfth Plane, ever since Wonk the Reformer, devouring fellow beings alive has been strictly forbidden. I supposed that the Prime Plane had similar regulations, although I had had no opportunity to master this world's many legal systems. I was comforted to think that, since I acted under Maldivius' orders, the responsibility would be his.

Doctor Maldivius returned late the next day. He asked: "Where is Grax?"

"Following your orders, master, I was compelled to devour him."

"*What?*"

"Aye, sir." I explained the circumstances.

"Imbecile!" shrieked the wizard, going for me with his wand again. "Fool! Dunce! Lout! Ass! Dolt! Blunderhead! What have I done to the gods that they should visit a jolthead like you upon me?"

He was chasing and whacking me all the while. I darted out of the chamber but got lost in the maze. As a result, Maldivius cornered me at the end of a blind passage and continued his beating until exhaustion forced him to stop.

"Mean you," I said at last, "that you did not intend me to eat this youth?"

"Of course I meant it!" *Whack*. "Any idiot could have seen that!"

"But, sir, you expressly commanded me—" And I went through the logic of the situation again.

Maldivius raked his gray hair back from his face and drew his sleeve across his forehead. "Beshrew me, but I suppose I ought to have known better. Come back to the chamber." When we reached the sanctum, he said: "Gather up those bones, tie them together, and throw them into the sea."

"I am sorry, sir; I did but try to give satisfaction. As we say in Ning, no one being can excel in everything. Will Grax's disappearance entail any legal consequences for you?"

"Not likely. He was a kinless orphan; that was why he wished to become my apprentice. If, however, you should be asked, say that he fell from the cliff and was carried off by some denizen of the deep. Now let us plan a proper dinner, for I expect an eminent visitor tomorrow."

"Who is this, master?"

"His Excellency Jimmon, the Chief Syndic of Ir. I made them an offer, but they derided it and suggested one tenth of my price as a just requital. Jimmon said he might drop by to discuss the matter further. This bids fair to be a lengthy haggle."

"Are you sure, sir, that the doom you foresee will not come upon the land whilst you and the Syndics chaffer? As we say on my plane, a fish in the creel is worth two in the stream."

"Nay, nay; I keep watch on this menace by my Sapphire. We have a plenty of time."

"Sir, may I ask what sort of menace this is?"

"You may ask, ha ha, but I won't answer. I know better than to—ah—let this bird out of its cage by blabbing what's known only to me. Now get to work."

His Excellency the Syndic Jimmon was a fat, bald man borne in a litter, who stayed overnight while his servants went to Chemnis for lodging. I did my best to play the perfect servant. I had been told to stand behind the chair of the guest at dinner, to anticipate his every wish.

Betimes, Jimmon and Maldivius haggled over the price of revealing Ir's doom, and betimes they gossiped about events in Ir. Jimmon said:

"If someone stop not that accursed woman, by Thio's horn, she'll attain the Board of Syndics yet."

"What of it?" said Maldivius. "Since your government is based upon wealth, and Madame Roska has the wealth, why should you mind her taking her seat amongst you?"

"We have never had a woman syndic; 'twere unprecedented. Moreover, everyone knows what a silly female she is."

"Ahem. Not too silly to multiply her fortune, methinks."

"By witchcraft, belike. 'Tis said she dabbles in wizardry. Humph. The word is out of joint, when a featherwitted frail can amass such lucre. But let us talk of pleasanter things. Have you seen Bagardo's traveling circus, eh? 'Twas in Ir last fiftnight, and meseems Bagardo the Great is now touring the smaller towns and villages. His entertainment is not bad. But if he come to Chemnis, beware that he fleece you not. Like all such mountebank, he's full of wiles and guile."

Maldivius chuckled. "He needs must arise early to fleece me and not—ah—the other way round. Stop your squirming, Your Excellency; my servant will not harm you. He is a very paragon of literal obedience."

"Then, wouldst mind asking him to stand behind your chair instead of mine? His looks disquiet me, and I'm getting a crick in my poor neck from craning it to view him."

Maldivius commanded me to change my place. I obeyed, albeit I found it hard to understand Jimmon's apprehensions. At home, I am deemed a perfectly average sort of demon, in no way outstanding or formidable.

The next day, Syndic Jimmon departed in his litter, bouncing on the shoulders of eight stalwart bearers. Maldivius told me: "Now understand once and for all, O Zdim, that your purpose in guarding my sanctum is not to slay anyone who happens by, but to forestall thievery. So you shall devour thieves and none other."

"But, master, how shall I know a thief?"

"By his actions, fool! If he seek to snatch some bauble of mine and make off with it, destroy him. But, if he be merely a customer wishing his horoscope cast, or a peddler with sundries for sale, or a villager from Chemnis who fain would exchange a sack of produce for aid in finding his wife's lost bangle, then seat him courteously and watch him closely until I return. But, unless he truly attempt to filch, *harm him not!* Have you got that through your adamantine skull?"

"Aye, sir."

For the next fortnight, little happened. I continued to cook and clean. Maldivius went once to Chemnis and once to Ir; Jimmon paid us one more visit. Maldivius and Jimmon continued their chaffer, inching towards each other's positions with snail-like sloth. At this rate, meseemed the predicted doom would have come and gone thrice over ere they reached agreement.

When not otherwise occupied, Maldivius consulted the Sibylline Sapphire. Since he insisted that I stand guard over him while he was in his vaticinatory trance, I soon learn his procedure. He prayed; he burnt a mixture of spicy herbs in a little brazier and inhaled the smoke; he chanted a spell in the Mulvanian tongue, beginning:

> *Jyū zormē barh tigai tyūvu;*
> *Jyū zormē barh tigau tyūvu . . .*

I could tell from a sensation in my tendrils when the spell began to take effect.

Having mastered my domestic tasks, I found time hanging heavily on my hands. We demons are far more patient than these fidgety Prime Planers; natheless, I found sitting hour upon hour in the sanctum, doing absolutely nothing, more than a little tedious. At length I asked:

"Master, might I take the liberty of reading one of your books whilst I wait?"

"Why," said Maldivius, "can you read Novarian?"

"I studied it in school, and—"

"Mean you that you have schools, too, on the Twelfth Plane?"

"Certes, sir. How else should we rear our young in the ways they should go?"

Maldivius: "And young as well? Somehow I have never heard of a young demon."

"Naturally, since we do not permit the immature of our kind to serve on the Prime Plane. It were too hazardous for them. I assure you that we are hatched, and grow, and die like other sentient creatures. But about your books: I see you have a lexicon to help with words I know not. I beg you to suffer me to use it."

"Hm, hm. Not a bad idea. When you become skilled enough, belike you can read aloud to me, as poor Grax was wont to do. At my age, I needs employ a reading glass, which makes reading a laborious business. What sort of book have you in mind?"

"I should like to start on this one, sir," I said, pulling out the copy of Voltiper's *Material and Spiritual Perfection in Ten Easy Lessons*. "Methinks I shall need all the perfection I can attain, to furnish satisfaction on this unfamiliar plane."

"Let me see that!" said he, snatching the book out of my claws. His old eyes—keen enough despite his words—had glimpsed the blots of blood that marred several pages. "A souvenir of poor Grax, eh? Lucky for you, O fiend, that the book is of no magical import. Take it, and may you profit from its advice."

So, with the help of Maldivius' lexicon, I began plowing through Voltiper of Kortoli. The second chapter was devoted to Voltiper's theories of diet. He was, it transpired, a vegetarian. He averred that only by eschewing the flesh of animals could the reader attain the sought-for perfect health and spiritual attunement with the cosmos. Voltiper also had moral objections to slaying sentient beings for food. He held that they had souls, even if rudimentary ones, and that they were akin to human beings as a result of evolutionary descent from common ancestors.

These moral arguments did not much concern me, since I was but a temporary resident of this plane. But I did wish better to adapt myself to the ways of the Prime Plane, to make my sojourn as painless as possible. I took up the vegetarian diet with Maldivius.

"A capital idea, Zdim," quoth he. "I once practiced such a regimen myself, but Grax was so insistent upon flesh that I weakly gave in to him. Let us both follow Voltiper's prescription. It will also abate our expenses."

So Maldivius and I ceased to buy meat at Chemnis and contented ourselves with bread and greens. Then the wizard said:

"O Zdim, the Sibylline Sapphire tells me that Bagardo's circus is coming to Chemnis. I shall go thither to witness the show and, incidentally, to put forth discreet inquiries for a successor to my whilom apprentice. Bide you here."

"I should like to see such a show, sir. I have been here for a month without stirring out of this ruin."

"What, *you* go to Chemnis? The gods forfend! I have it hard enough, keeping on the good side of the townspeople, without your scaring them out of their wits."

Since there was no help for it, I saddled up the mule, watched my master out of sight, and returned to the sanctum.

Hours later, a sound distracted me from my reading. It seemed to come from above. Whereas the brass lamps did not strongly illumine the ceiling, I could easily see that a large, quadrilateral hole had appeared in the plaster. How the intruder lifted that oblong of plaster out of the way without breaking it or arousing me sooner I know not. The burglarious sleights of Prime Planers are too subtle for the simple, straightforward mind of an honest demon.

I sat, watching. Demons have the advantage over human beings of being able to remain truly motionless. A Prime Planer, even when he tries to hold still, is al-

ways moving and fidgeting. If nought else gives him
away, the fact that he must needs breathe several times
a minute will. The fact that we can change color, too,
gives Prime Planers exaggerated notions of our powers—as the belief that we can vanish at will.

A rope came dangling down through the hole, and
down this rope came a small man in dark, close-fitting
garb. By happenstance, he had his back to me as he
lowered himself. His first brief glance failed to note me,
sitting quietly in my chair, matching my background
and not even breathing. Like a frightened mouse, he
scuttled on soundless soft shoes to the stand holding
the Sibylline Sapphire.

Instanter, I was out of my chair and upon him. He
snatched the gem and whirled. For a heartbeat we con-
fronted each other, he with the gemstone in hand and
me with fangs bared, ready to tear him apart and devour him.

But then I recalled Voltiper's insistence on vegetari-
anism and Maldivius' orders to follow Voltiper's die-
tary advice. Such being the case, I could obviously
not devour the thief. On the other hand, my master
had given me express commands to eat any flagrant
robber.

Given these contradictory orders, I found myself
palsied as surely as if I had been packed in ice and
frozen stiff. With the best intentions, I could only stand
like a stuffed beast in a museum while the thief darted
around me and out, drawing from his wallet a tube full
of glowworms to light his way.

After I had earnestly pondered these things for
several minutes, it occurred to me what, belike,
Maldivius would have wished me to do, had he known
the full circumstances. This would have been to seize
the thief, take the Sapphire from him, and hold him
against the wizard's return. I think this was very clever
of me. Of course, Prime Planers are much quicker of
wit than we demons, and it is unfair to expect us to be
so nimble-witted as they.

Alas, my solution came too late. I ran out of the
maze and raced up the cliffside stair. By this time,
however, there was no sign of Master Thief. I could

not even hear his retreating footsteps. I cast about to try to pick up his odor but failed to strike a definite trail. The gem had gone for good.

When Doctor Maldivius returned and learnt the news, he did not even beat me. He sat down, covered his face with his hands, and wept. At last he wiped his eyes and looked up, saying:

"O Zdim, I see that commanding you to cope with unforeseen contingencies is like—ah—like asking a horse to play the fiddle. Well, even if I be ruined, I need not compound my folly by retaining your bungling services."

"Mean you, sir, that I shall be dismissed back to my own plane?" I asked eagerly.

"Certes, no! The least I can do to recover my loss is to sell your contract. I know just the customer, too."

"What mean you, to sell my contract?"

"If you read the agreement betwixt the Government of Ning and the Forces of Progress—as we Novarian wizards call our professional society—you will see that indentures are explicitly made transferable. I have a copy here somewhere." He fumbled in a chest.

"I protest, sir!" I cried. "That is no better than slavery!"

Maldivius straightened up with a scroll, which he unrolled and held to the lamplight.

"See you what it says here? And here? If you mislike these terms, take the matter up with your Provost at the end of your indenture. What did this thief look like?"

I described the fellow, mentioning such things as the small scar on his right cheek, which no mere Prime Planer would ever have noticed during a glimpse by lamplight.

"That would be Farimes of Hendau," said Maldivius. "I knew him of old, when I dwelt in Ir. Well, saddle up Rosebud again. I am for Chemnis the night."

The wizard left me in no very pleasant mood. I am a patient demon—infinitely more so than these hasty, headstrong human beings—but I could not help feeling that Doctor Maldivius was treating me unjustly. Twice in a row he had laid all the blame for our disasters on me, when it was his fault for issuing vague and contradictory orders.

I was tempted to use my decamping spell, to flit back to the Twelfth Plane and bring my complaints before the Provost. This spell is taught us ere we leave our own plane, so that we can return to it on the instant when threatened by imminent destruction. It is not to be used frivolously, for which use the penalties are severe. The fact that a demon can vanish when human beings are about to slay him has given Prime Planers overblown ideas of our powers.

The decamping spell, however, is long and complicated. When I tried to run over it in my mind, I found I had forgotten several lines and was therefore, trapped on the Prime Plane. Perhaps it is just as well, for I might have been convicted of frivolous use of the spell and sent back to the Prime Plane under sentence of several years of indenture. And that had been just too dreadful a fate.

Maldivius returned next morning with another man. Mounted on a fine piebald horse, the other man was clad in dashing, gaudy style compared with the somber, patched, and threadbare garments of my master. He was a man of early middle age, thin in the legs but massive in arms and body. He shaved his face but seemed to be fighting a losing battle against a thick heavy, blue-black beard. Golden hoops dangled from his ears.

"This," said Maldivius, "is your new master, Bagardo the Great. Master Bagardo, meet Demon Zdim."

Bagardo stared me up and down. "He does look sound of wind and limb, albeit 'tis hard to judge an unfamiliar species. Well, Doctor, if you'll show me the paper, I will sign."

And that is how I became an indentured servant of Bagardo the Great, proprietor of a traveling carnival.

III

BAGARDO THE GREAT

"COME with me," said Bagardo. As I followed him, he went on: "Let me get your name right. Za-dim, is that it?"

"Nay, Zdim," I said. "One syllable. Zdim son of Akh, if you would be formal."

Bagardo practiced the name. I asked: "What will be my duties, sir?"

"Mainly, to scare the marks."

"Sir? I understand not."

"Marks, rubes, shills are what we circus folk call the customers who come to gawp." (Bagardo always called his establishment a "circus," although others alluded to it as a "carnival." The difference, I learnt, was that a true circus needs must have at least one elephant, whereas Bagardo had none.) "You will be put in a traveling cage and introduced as the terrible man-eating demon from the Twelfth Plane. And that's no lie, from what Maldivius tells me."

"Sir, I did but carry out my orders—"

"Never mind. I'll try to give more exact commands."

We came to where the track from the temple joined the road from Chemnis to Ir. Here stood a large, iron-barred cage on wheels, like a wagon. Hitched to the wagon, grazing, were a pair of animals like Maldivius' mule, save that they were covered with gaudy black-and-white stripes. On the driver's seat lolled a squat, lowbrowed, chinless creature, naked but for his thick, hairy pelt, like a man and yet not like a man.

"Is all well?" said Bagardo.

"All's well, boss," said the thing in a deep, croaking voice. "Who this?"

"A new member of our troupe, hight Zdim the

22

Demon," quoth Bagardo. "Zdim, meet Ungah of Komilakh. He's what we call an ape-man."

"Shake, fellow slave," said Ungah, putting out a hairy paw.

"Shake?" said I, looking a question at Bagardo. "Like this, does he mean?" I twitched my hips back and forth.

Bagardo said: "Clasp his right hand in yours and squeeze gently whilst moving the hands up and down. Don't claw him."

I did so, saying: "I am gratified to make your acquaintance, Master Ungah. I am not a slave, but an indentured servant."

"Lucky losel! I must swink for Master Bagardo till death us part."

"You're better fed than you ever would be in the jungles of Komilakh, you know," said Bagardo.

"Aye, master; but food is not all."

"What, then? But we can't argue all day." Bagardo threw open the door of the cage. "Get in," he said.

The door closed with a clang. I sat down on a large wooden chest at one end of the cage. Bagardo swung up on the driver's seat behind Ungah, who clucked and shook the reins. The wagon lurched off to westward.

The road zigzagged down a long slope into the valley of the Kyamos River, which runs from Metouro across Ir to the sea. Another hour brought us in sight of Chemnis at the rivermouth. This is a small town by Prime Plane standards, but a busy one, for it is the main port of Ir. Over the roofs I saw the masts and yards of ships.

On the outskirts, a cluster of tents, gay with pennons, marked Bagardo's carnival. As the wagon turned into the field, I saw a score of men laboring to strike these tents and pack them into wagons. Others hitched horses to these wagons. The clatter and shouting could have been heard leagues away.

As my cage-wagon drew to a halt, Bagardo leapt down from his perch. "Ye idiots! Loafers! Idle witlings!" he yelled. "We should have been ready to roll by now! Can you do nought without me to command you? How shall we ever reach Evrodium by tomorrow

night? Ungah, cease your insolent grinning, you bare-
arsed ape! Get down and get to work! Let Zdim out;
we need every hand."

The ape-man obediently descended and opened my
door. As I issued from the cage, some of the others
looked at me askance. They were, however, used to ex-
otic creatures and soon returned to their tasks.

Ungah busied himself with lashing a sheet of canvas
around a bundle of stakes. He handed me one end of
the rope and said:

"Hold this. When I say pull, pull!"

On signal, I pulled. The rope broke, so that I fell
backward and got my tail muddy. Ungah looked at the
broken ends of the rope with a puzzled frown.

"This rope seems sound," he said. "Must be you're
stronger than I thought."

He tied the broken ends together and resumed his
task, warning me not to exert my full force. By the
time we had the bundle lashed and stowed, the main
tent had come down and the workmen were cleaning
up the last pieces of equipment. I could not but marvel
how, despite the frightful confusion that had obtained
before, everything was packed up at last. Bagardo, now
mounted on his horse and wearing a trumpet on a cord
around his neck, waved a wide-brimmed hat to em-
phasize his commands:

"Yare with that harness! Siglar, run your cat wagon
up to the gate; I'm putting you at the head. Ungah, put
Zdim back into his wagon and pull into line . . ."

"Back you go," said Ungah to me. When I was in
the cage, he untied the lashings of a pair of canvas
rolls on the sides of the roof, so that the canvas fell
down on both sides of the wagon. Since the ends of the
cage were solid, I was cut off from the outside.

"Ho!" I cried. "Why are you shutting me in?"

"Orders," said Ungah, tying down the lower edges
of the curtains. "Boss would not give Chemnites a free
show."

"But I am fain to see the countryside!"

"Be at ease, Master Zdim. When we get into open
country, I'll pull up a corner of your sheets."

Bagardo blew a shrill tucket. With a vast noise of

cracking whips, neighing horses, clattering hooves, jingling harness, creaking axles, shouts, curses, warnings, jests, and snatches of song, the wagons lurched into motion. I could see nought, so for the first hour I settled into a digestive torpor, lolling and swaying on the wooden chest.

At length, I called out to remind Ungah of his promise. At a halt to breathe the horses, he untied the forward lower corner of one curtain and tied it up, affording me a three-sided window. I saw little but farmers' fields, with now and then a patch of forest or a glimpse of the Kyamos. The road was lined by a dense belt of spring wildflowers, in clusters of crimson, azure, purple, white, and gold.

When a bend in the road permitted, I saw the rest of the train before and behind. I counted seventeen wagons including my own. Bagardo cantered from one end of the line to the other, making sure that all went well.

We followed the road by which I had come to Chemnis. We climbed to the plateau whereon the temple stands, since the vale of the Kyamos here narrows to a gorge. The horses plodded slowly up the grade, while the workmen got out to push.

When we reached the plateau and passed the jointure with the path to the temple of Psaan, the road leveled and we went faster. We did not continue towards Ir but turned off on another road, which bypassed the capital to the south. As Ungah explained, we had milked Ir lately and her udder had not had time to refill.

We had covered less than half the distance to Evrodium when night descended upon us. The wagon train pulled off the road on an unplowed stretch of flatland, and the seventeen wagons formed a rough circle—for defense, Ungah told me, in the event of attack by marauders. The cook's tent and the dining tent were set up inside the circle, but the other tents were left in their wagons.

We ate by yellow lamplight at one of a number of tables in the long dining tent, together with fifty-odd other members of the troupe. Ungah pointed out individuals. Half were roustabouts—workers who did such chores as erecting and striking the tents; harnessing, driving, and unhitching the horses; fetching food and water to the beasts; and carrying off their dung.

Of the rest of the company, half—a quarter of the total—were gamesters: that is, men who, for a rental fee, accompanied the carnival and plied their games with the public. These games entailed wagers on such things as the roll of dice, the turns of a wheel of fortune, or the location of a pea beneath one of three nutshells, all nicely contrived for the undoing of artless marks.

This left a mere sixteen or so performers, who appeared before the audiences. These comprised Bagardo himself, as ringmaster; a snake charmer; a lion tamer; a bareback rider; a dog trainer; a juggler; two clowns; three acrobats; four musicians (a drummer, a trumpeter, a fiddler, and a bagpiper); and an animal handler who, clad as a Mulvanian prince in turban and glass jewels, rode around the ring on the camel. There were also a cook and a costumer. These last, together with the snake charmer and the bareback rider, were women.

The company was more versatile than this list implies. Most of these folk doubled at other tasks: thus the snake charmer helped the cook to serve repasts, while the bareback rider—a buxom wench clept Dulnessa—assisted the costumer in cutting and stitching. Some roustabouts, seeking to work their way into better-paying jobs, betimes took the stead of performers when the latter were sick, drunk, or otherwise out of action.

After dinner, Ungah took me the rounds of the carnival, presenting me to individuals and showing me the exhibits. These included the camel, the lion, the leopard, and several smaller beasts such as Madam Paladné's snakes.

Ungah approached one long cage on wheels with caution. I sensed a distinctive odor about the cage, like that of Madam Paladné's serpents but stronger. Ungah pulled back the curtain.

" 'Tis the Paaluan dragon," he said. "Go not close, Zdim. It lies like dead thing for a fiftnight; then when

some unwary wight comes too close: *snap!* And that is
end of him. That's why Bagardo has trouble getting
the roustabouts to service the brute; have lost two men
to its maw in last year."

The dragon was a great, slate-colored lizard, over
twenty feet long. As we neared the cage, it raised its
head and shot a yard of forked tongue at me. I stepped
close, trusting in my quickness to leap out of harm's
way if it snapped. Instead, the dragon extended that
tongue again and touched my face with a caressing motion. A wheezy grunt came from its throat.

"By Vaisus' brazen arse!" cried Ungah. "It *likes*
you! It knows your smell as that of fellow reptile. Must
tell Bagardo. Belike you could train the creature and
ride about ring on it with the rest of parade. It seems
stupid, and nobody had dared to meddle with it since
Xion was et; but black wizards of Paalua train these
beasts."

"It is a mickle of a monster for me to handle alone,"
I said doubtfully.

"Oh, this one only half grown," said Ungah. "In
Paalua, they get twice as big." He yawned. "Back to
wagon; am fordone with today's stint."

At the wagon, Ungah took a pair of blankets out of
his chest and handed me one, saying: "Straw in bottom
of the chest, if you find the floor too hard."

The next day's sun had set when we came to Evrodium. The caravan's halting place was lit by torches
and lanthorns, which shone on the eyeballs of a swarm
of villagers standing about the margin of the lot.

"Zdim!" cried Ungah. "Bear hand!"

He unrolled the canvas I had helped him tie up. Inside was a bundle of stakes longer than I am tall. Our
task was to drive these stakes at intervals into the
ground and attach the canvas to them, to enclose the
carnival and thwart the curious locals who wished to
see but not pay. Ungah chose a place on the perimeter
of the lot and pushed the first stake into the soft
ground. He set a small stepladder behind it and pressed
the handle of a mallet into my hand.

"Get up there and drive stake in," he directed.

I mounted the stepladder and gave the stake a tap.

"Hit hard!" cried Ungah. "Is that your best?"

"Mean you thus?" quoth I, swinging the mallet with full force. It came down with a crash, splintering the top of the stake and breaking the handle of the mallet.

"Zevatas, Franda, and Heryx!" yelled Ungah. "Meant not to smash it to kindling. Now must fetch another mallet. Wait here!"

One way or another, we got the canvas fence up. Meanwhile, the tents had been erected and the early confusion had subsided into an orderly bustle. Horses neighed, the camel gargled, the lion roared, and the other beasts made their proper noises. I asked:

"Shall we put on a show tonight?"

"Gods, no! Takes hours to get ready, and everybody too tired. We pass the morn in preparation and, if rain hold off, do one show. Then off on the road again."

"Wherefore pause we here so briefly?"

"Evrodium too small. By tomorrow night, all marks with money have seen the performance, and game players be cleaned out. Stay longer means battle with the marks. No profit in that." A gong sounded. "Dinner! Come along."

We were up with the dawn, readying the day's performance. Bagardo came to see me.

"O Zdim," he said, "you shall be in the tent of monsters—"

"Your pardon, master, but I am no monster! I am but a normal, healthy—"

"Never mind! With us, you shall be a monster, and no back talk. Your wagon will form part of the wall of the tent, and the marks will move past it on the inner side. Ungah will be next to you. Since you occupy his cage, I'll chain him to a post. Your task is to fright the marks with hideous roars and howls. Speak no words of Novarian. You're not supposed to know how, you know."

"But sir, I not only speak it, I read and write—"

"Look here, demon, who's running this circus? You shall do as told, like it or not."

And so it befell. The villagers turned out in mass.

From my cage, I heard the cries of the gamesters and the rattle of their devices, the tunes of the musical band, and the general uproar. Bagardo, splendidly attired, ushered a host of marks in with a florid oration:

". . . and first on your right, messires and mesdames, you see Madame Paladné and her deadly serpents, captured at inconceivable risk in the reeking tropical jungles of Mulvan. The large one is clept a constrictor. Were it to seize you, it would wrap you round, crush you to a jelly, and swallow you whole . . . Next, messires and mesdames, is a demon from the Twelfth Plane, evoked by the great warlock, Arkanius of Phthai. I knew Arkanius; in fact, he was a dear friend." Bagardo wiped his eyes with a kerchief. "But in evoking this bloodthirsty monster of supernatural strength and ferocity, he left a corner of his pentacle open, and the demon bit his head off."

Some of the audience gasped, and a few of the women uttered small shrieks. A mark, in a rustic accent I could scarcely understand, asked:

"How didst tha take him, then?"

"Arkanius' apprentice bravely cast a spell of immobility . . ."

I was so fascinated by Bagardo's account of my past that I forgot to roar until he scowled at me. Then I champed my jaws, hopped up and down, and did such other antics as seemed called for.

Bagardo gave an equally fictional account of the capture of Ungah, who sat on the ground chained to a post, behind a railing to keep the marks at a safe distance from his clutches. When the marks gathered at the railing, Ungah grimaced, roared and slapped a sheet of iron with a length of chain, making a much more impressive racket than had I.

After the performance, Bagardo unchained Ungah and opened my cage. Ungah entered the cage and dug out of the chest a huge, moth-eaten old cloak, a battered hat with a floppy brim, a pair of gap-toed boots, a belt, and a purse. He did on all these things.

"Wherefore the fine raiment, Master Ungah?" I asked.

"Boss insists. Go to Evrodium to buy things. When the light fails, villagers take me for roustabout. If they see Ungah the Terrible talking polite, they wouldn't pay to see me in tent. You want anything?"

"I know of nought at the moment. But tell me: What do you buy with?"

"Money. Bagardo gives me allowance."

An hour later, Ungah returned with his purchases: some sweetmeats, which he shared with me; a needle, thread, and scissors; and other things. After dinner, Ungah was patching his cloak by lamplight when Siglar, the lion tamer, approached our cage. Siglar, a tall bony man with pale-blue eyes and lank, tow-colored hair, was a barbarian from the steppes of Shven to the north.

"Master Zdim!" he said. "The boss is fain to see you."

I suspected that Bagardo would complain about my lackluster performance. I said to Ungah: "Couldst accompany me, old fellow? I need moral support."

Ungah put away his sewing and came. We wended to Bagardo's small private wagon. Inside, the vehicle was luxuriously fitted up with silken drapes, a thick rug, and a silver-gilt lamp to shine upon this splendor.

Bagardo was seated at his desk, casting his accounts with a slate and a piece of chalk. "O Zdim!" he said. "In twenty years in this business, never have I seen a worse performance than yours. Briefly, you stink."

"I am sorry, master; I endeavor to give satisfaction, but to please everybody were oft impossible. If you paid me an allowance, I might be inspired to a more vital act."

"Oho, so that's it? With the circus teetering on the edge of failure and the entire company's pay in arrears, you strike me for pay. A murrain on you, demon!" He smote the desk so that his inkwell danced.

"Very well, sir," I replied. "I will do my best; but, in my state of destitution, that best may not be very good."

"Insolent ouph!" roared Bagardo. "I'll destitute you!" He came around the desk with the small whip that he cracked as ringmaster. He took a cut at me, and another. Since this was no magical wand, I scarcely felt the blows.

"Is that the hardest you can hit, sir?" I said.

He struck me a few more times, then hurled the whip into a corner. "Curse you, are you made of iron?"

"Not quite, sir. It is true that my tissues are stronger than yours. Now, how about that allowance? As we Twelfth Planers say, every pump needs a little priming betimes."

Red-faced, Bagardo glared. Then he laughed. "Oh, all right; you do have me by the balls, you know. How about threepence a day?"

"That were agreeable, master. Now, could I but have a few days' advance for pocket money . . ."

Bagardo brought ninepence out of his strongbox. "That'll have to do for the next fiftnight. Enough of sordid commercialism; who's for a game of skillet?"

"What is that, sir?" I asked.

"You shall see." Bagardo set out a small table and four folding chairs. As Siglar, Ungah, and I took our places, Bagardo produced a package of oblongs of stiff paper with designs upon them. Prime Planers play a multitude of games with these "cards," as they call them.

The rules of skillet seemed simple. Various combinations of cards outranked others, and the trick was to guess the other players' hands and wager on one's ability to outrank them. I had a terrible time in managing the cards with my claws, which are not suited to such slippery objects. I kept dropping the wretched things on the floor.

Bagardo kept up a fire of talk. He boasted grandly of his prowess in fertilizing the females of his species. He was especially proud of having copulated with six inmates of an institution called a whorehouse, all in one night. I was puzzled by the pride that male Prime Planers take in this ability, since any number of lower animals, such as the common goat, can easily outdo the human male in this regard.

When all had lauded Bagardo's penial powers, he

said: "Zdim, since you arrived on this plane, have you known any wizards other than Doc Maldivius?"

"Nay, sir, save for his apprentice Grax, who—ah—met with misfortune. Why?"

"We need one. We had one, old Arkanius."

"I heard you mention him, sir. What really befell him?"

"Something not greatly different from the lies I told about him, I'll warrant. Arkanius would experiment with spells too fell for his limited powers. One night we saw blue flashes from his tent and heard screams. On the morrow there was no Arkanius—just a spattering of blood. I offered the job to Maldivius, but he declined, uttering something about the Paaluans making his fortune for him. He was a bit drunk at the time. Know you aught of what he meant?"

"Nay, sir. I have heard that Paalua is a land of mighty magicians across the ocean, but that is all."

"Bear it in mind. Dulnessa has been running a fortune-telling booth besides her regular work, but 'tis not the same as having a genuine magicker, you know. Whose deal is it?"

Bagardo won my ninepence away from me, coin by coin. I noted that, from time to time, my tendrils picked up a strange vibration. This often happened when he was about to win some of my money. I could not, however, properly interpret the sensation. When I was down to my last farthing, the door opened and in came the buxom Madam Dulnessa, the bareback rider. In a raucous voice, she cried:

"When is one of you limp-yards coming over to service me?"

Bagardo said: "Take Zdim. He's broke, anyway."

"Mean you he *can*?" she said.

"Certes. Demons engender even as we do. Now get thee hence and leave us to our play."

Perplexed, I followed Dulnessa back to her wagon. When we were inside, she turned to me with a smile and half-closed eyes.

"Well, Zdimmy," she said, "this bids fair to be at least a new sensation."

With that, she began to remove her clothing in a slow and provocative manner. When she had doffed all her garments, she lay supine on her bed. I was naturally interested, since this was my first view of a live human female without clothing. I was gratified to observe that the illustrations in the schoolbooks on my own plane were correct in their depiction of the form and organs of this species. My tendrils received a vibration of extraordinary intensity, which I did not recognize.

"Now go to it, if you have the means to go to it with," she said.

I began to see. "Mean you to engage in carnal communication with you, madam?"

"Whoops, what pretty language! Aye, I mean just that."

"I am sorry, but I was taught only the refined, literary form of Novarian in school. The vulgarisms I have had to pick up on my own."

"Well, have you in sooth a true member under all those scales—and, hey, you're changing color!"

"Emotion so affects us, madam. I assure you that I am equipped with a proper male organ. Amongst us, however, it is withdrawn within the body when not in use, instead of dangling vulgarly and vulnerably as amongst human males. Doubtless that is the cause of this curious custom—which has long puzzled our philosophers—of wearing garments, even in the hottest weather. Now, amongst us demons—"

Dulnessa: "Spare me the lecture. Canst do it?"

"I know not. Although I strive to give satisfaction, this is not the breeding season, nor does the site of a Prime Planc female arouse my desires."

"What's the matter with me, dragon-man? True, I'm not so young as once upon a time, but—"

"That is beside the point, if you will pardon my saying so, madam. With that soft, pale, nude skin all over, you look—how shall I say it?—squashy. It were like copulating with a giant jellyfish, ugh! Now if it were my wife Yeth, with her pretty fangs and tendrils and her lovely, glittering scales—"

"Then close your eyes, fancy 'tis your wife lying here, and try to work up a stand."

Well, as we say at home, nought essayed, nought achieved. By a powerful effort of will, I envisaged my dear mate and felt the blood rush into my loins. When I was sure I was an upstanding demon, I opened my eyes.

Dulnessa was staring at my yard with horror. "My gods!" she cried. "Put that ghastly thing away! It looks like one of those spiky maces that knights bash in each other's armor with. 'Twould slay me dead."

"I regret not to be of service to you, madam," I said. "I feared you would not find the prospect pleasing. Now why should Master Bagardo have sent me with you? It seems like one of those irrational 'jokes' that you human beings are ever perpetrating. If Bagardo had lust enough for a score of women, I should think he were glad of the opportunity——"

"That bully-rook talks fine, but his performance fails to match his brag. The last time, he had to call on Siglar to take his place after one gallop. The ape-man's worth three of him on a pallet."

"Do all human females require such constant replenishment?"

"Nay; I'm a special case. Because I wouldn't let him make free with me, the cursed Arkanius cast a spell upon me——the spell of unrequited lust. He was a dirty old lob, and I joyed when the demon fanged him. But that leaves me under the spell, with no wizard to lift it."

"Perhaps it will wear off in time," I said. "Spells do, I understand."

"Maybe so; but meanwhile, if I be not well stroked several times daily, my desire drives me mad."

"I should think, with all these lusty roustabouts——"

"Most never bathe, and I prefer cleanly lovers. Still, if all else fail . . . But to get back to your game. How fared you?"

I told of my loss.

"Ha!" she said. " 'Tis like Bagardo to advance you money and then get it back by card-sharping."

"Mean you he cheated me?"

"Certes! What thought you?"

I pondered. "That must be the meaning of that tingle I sensed."

"Canst read minds?"

"Nay, but I detect vibrations that betray the emotions of other beings."

"How much does he pay you?"

"Threepence a day."

She laughed hoarsely. "My dear Zdim, you go right back to Bagardo and make him double it; he pays the roustabouts sixpence. Then borrow another advance and win back your poke. That will be the right sort of joke on that great coystrill!"

I did as bidden. Bagardo laughed heartily at the tale of Dulnessa's abortive seduction. It put him in such a good humor, in fact, that he even agreed to the rise in my pay, doubtless counting on speedily winning it back.

We resumed the game. By dropping out instantly every time I felt the warning tingle, I soon had won back several times the original advance. Bagardo stared, saying:

"I must be losing my card sense. Anyway, 'tis time we were abed. We needs must rise early to get to Orynx, you know. I maun say, Master Zdim, you have mastered skillet the quickest of anyone I've taught. Are you in some sort a mind reader?"

"Nay, master." My reply was truthful if "mind" be taken in the strictest sense, as comprising only the intellectual faculties; but some might take philosophical exception to it on the ground that the term should be extended to include the emotions, which I could in fact read. I went on: "The principles are not difficult. As we say in my world, perfection waits upon practice."

"Too bad you don't read minds; I could use you in an act. At the next show, now, remember: when the customers flock in, go into a veritable frenzy. They expect it. Roar, howl, shake the bars as if you would leap down amongst the marks. Strive your utmost to escape from the cage!"

Ungah said: "Boss, I think—"

"Never mind your thoughts, Master Ape. I would make sure this demon knows his script."

Orynx, up the Kyamos from Ir, is larger than Evrodium, albeit smaller than Chemnis. We planned to spend two full days there and to give three performances: two of evenings and one on the second afternoon. We opened the first show on the even of the first day.

The first mark to enter the tent of monsters was an old man with a wobbling gait. From the odor of wine he emitted, I inferred that his unsteadiness was due not merely to age. He staggered up to my wagon and peered. I returned his gaze, not wishing to go into my ferocity act until I had garnered a larger audience.

The aged man took a bottle out of his coat and drank. He muttered: "Dip me in dung, and now a see them everywhere. Go away, spook! Evanish! Get tha gone! O gods, ask me ne to give up me drink, me old man's milk, me one remaining solace!"

He reeled away, weeping, and other rubes streamed in. When Bagardo had given his turgid introductions, I growled, roared, screamed, and beat on the bars. Remembering my orders, I seized two bars and pulled them until they bent.

The nearest marks recoiled, while those further back pressed forward. Bagardo flashed me a grin of approval. Thus encouraged, I gave forth a bellow like that of a turtle-dragon of the Marshes of Kshak and put forth my full strength.

The bars bowed outward. With a loud snapping sound, one pulled out of its lower socket. I tore it out of its upper socket as well and cast it clattering from me. Then, as instructed, I squeezed through the gap and leapt to the ground, roaring and snatching at the nearest marks.

I had no intention of harming the customers; I merely essayed to put on a good show. But the marks in front hurled themselves back with piercing screams. In a trice, the floor of the tent was a shambles of struggling bodies. Prime Planers fought and scrambled and fell over one another in their haste to get out, shrieking: "The fiend's loose!"

As they poured out into the night, their panic spread to others, who were streaming in the gate and towards the main tent. I have never witnessed such irrational behavior on the Twelfth Plane. We may be slow of wit, but an unwelcome surprise does not drive us insane.

Some people tried to climb over or burrow under the canvas fence around the lot. Those who had been knocked down and trampled limped or crawled towards the exit. Fights broke out. Some of the gamesters' booths were upset, and townsfolk began looting them. A tent blazed up. Somebody shouted: "Hey, rube!" Thereupon the roustabouts fell upon the marks with tent stakes or any other weapon they could improvise.

The deafening noise died down as all the marks who could still do so fled. Many lay hurt or unconscious about the lot. I glimpsed Bagardo, muddy and battered, staggering about and trying to bring his company to order. Seeing me, he yelled:

"You've ruined me, you lousy spook! I'll kill you for this!"

Others ran between us, and I lost sight of him. I followed Ungah in fighting the fire of the burning tent. By the time we had it out, a man wearing a helmet, a mail shirt, and a sword appeared on horseback at the entrance. A score of locals with crossbows, spears, and staves followed him afoot. The mounted man blew a trumpet.

"Who in the forty-nine hells are you?" said Bagardo, confronting the horse with fists on hips.

"Valtho, constable of Orynx. These be my deputies. Now hear this! Ye do all be under arrest for injuries done the citizens of Orynx. Ye face criminal charges and civil suits. Since our gaol would ne hold so many, ye shall remain here under guard this night—ho, whither go ye, sirrah? Stop that man!"

Bagardo ran back among the tents. Before any could catch him, he had thrown himself upon the piebald horse and kicked it to a gallop. He raced through the scattering carnival folk.

The horse soared over the fence, and Bagardo was gone into the night. Constable Valtho shouted an order to his men, who began to spread out and surround the lot, and spurred clattering after Bagardo. Several carnival folk ran off into the dark, to cut their way through the fence before the circle closed. I said to Ungah:

"Ought we not to flee, too?"

"Why? Can't get along on our own, for every man be against us. Best we can hope for is better masters. So take it easy."

Presently the constable came back from his fruitless pursuit of the showman, his horse puffing and blowing, to superintend the posting of his men. In the panic, one man had perished. This was the old drunkard, trampled to death at the entrance to the tent of monsters. There were many injuries, such as broken limbs and ribs. Besides these, every Oryncian who had even been jostled or gotten a spot on his coat had filed suit against Bagardo the Great. Had Bagardo been master of ten carnivals, each more prosperous than this one, he still could never have satisfied all the judgments against him. Had he not fled, he had probably ended in debt slavery.

Before the magistrate in Orynx, I explained that I was not really a bloodthirsty monster but just a poor indentured demon trying to follow his master's orders.

"You do not sound like a fiend," said the magistrate. "On the other hand, you are not human, so destroying you were no murder. Many citizens favor that measure for their own protection."

"Permit me to say that they might find my destruction difficult, Your Honor," I told him, "as anyone who has dealt with the Twelfth Plane will tell you. Moreover, I can forestall such a fate by returning to my own plane." (I was bluffing, having forgotten part of the decamping spell.) "So long as no extreme measure be attempted, however, I am fain to coöperate with the good people of Orynx in obeying their laws and meeting my obligations."

The magistrate—one of the few reasonable Prime Planers I met—agreed that I ought to be given a

chance. About half the company had escaped from the
lot ere it was surrounded. The members of the troupe
who had been captured had so few possessions, that,
rather than support them in idleness in the gaol, the
magistrate let them go with warnings.

The animals, including Ungah and myself, and the
wagons, tents, and other properties were gathered, in-
ventoried, and sent down the road to Ir to be sold. The
auction was a dreary business, and I doubt if the
plaintiffs in Orynx got a farthing to the mark on their
claims. But that is how my contract of indenture was
bought, at the auction ground outside the city, by an
agent for Madam Roska of Ir.

IV

MADAM ROSKA

IR is a peculiar city, lying at the edge of a cluster of
hills beside a small tributary of the Kyamos, the
Vomantikon. Save for the huge cylindrical tower surrounding the entrance, it is built entirely underground.
It was conceived as a stronghold by Ardyman the Terrible, when he sought to unite all twelve Novarian nations under his rule. Finding a mass of solid granite in
the hills of Ir, he caused the city to be dug into the
mountainside, with tunnels and caverns serving the offices of streets and houses.

When Madam Roska's agent, Noïthen, had tucked
my contract of indenture into his doublet, he said:
"Come along, O Zdim. We wait upon my mistress."

A short, gorbellied man, Master Noïthen led me to
the tower. This was a structure of well-fitted granite
ashlars, over a hundred feet wide and thrice as great in
diameter. A ramp, wide enough for a laden wagon,
wound spirally about the cylinder, going up in such

wise that he who ascended had his right or unshielded side towards the wall.

A third of the way up, the ramp ended at a huge portal, with valves made of whole tree trunks squared and held together with bronzen brackets. This portal now stood open. From the platform whereon it looked, a narrow, spiral stair continued up around the tower for one complete turn, ending at a higher and smaller door.

The castellated upper rim of the tower was higher yet. The booms of catapults projected out over the edge. The roof also upheld a complicated structure, which I saw from afar but did not understand until I had followed Noïthen through the main portal, past a pair of tall, blond guards.

"Who are those fellows?" I asked Noïthen. "They look not like Novarians."

"Mercenaries from Shven. We are no warmongers, but a nation of peaceful farmers and merchants. Hence we hire the Shvenites to do our bloodletting for us. In peacetime, as now, they serve as our civic guard and police."

Inside the portal, a spacious circular courtyard, open to the sky, filled the center of the tower. Around the walls, a series of huge casemates, upheld by arcades, provided space for the city's defenders and their equipment. Above the topmost of these rows of chambers rose the ring-shaped roof whereon stood the catapults.

There also arose the structure I had seen from without. It was a huge mirror on a clockwork mounting, so that it followed the course of the sun during the day. In planning his city, Ardyman had slighted the problem of ventilation. To see in their burrows, the Irians had to burn lamps and candles, and to cook they had to burn fuel. The smoke and soot of these fires distressed them, to say nothing of the vitiation of the air. Furthermore, this condition worsened as the city grew and its galleries extended farther and farther into Mount Ir.

At last, an ingenious syndic persuaded the people to install a system of lighting by reflected sunlight. This at least made lamps superfluous on sunny days. The main mirror, mounted atop Ardyman's Tower, cast the sun's beams down into the courtyard, whence another mirror reflected them down the main street—Ardyman Avenue—of Ir. Smaller mirrors diverted the rays down side-streets and thence into individual dwellings.

When I speak of cave dwellings, do not envisage a natural cavern, bedight with stalactites and inhabited by a handful of skin-clad primitives. Ir City had been hewn from the rock by the ablest Novarian masons. Its aspect, save for the roof of rock overhead in place of sky, was not unlike that of any rich city of the Prime Plane.

The house fronts, which reached up to this stone roof, were like other house fronts. The masons had even carved lines on them to simulate the joints between the bricks or stones of ordinary houses. Since the structure was one solid mass of rock, these carvings served no useful purpose save to make the scene look more familiar.

Most of the dwellings of Ir were on the same level as the courtyard of Ardyman's Tower. There were other levels, above and below the main one, but these had been built after the original. As we wound our way along Ardyman Avenue, through the passing throngs, Noïthen asked:

"Were you not once indentured to Maldivius the diviner?"

"Aye, sir. He evoked me from my own plane and later sold my contract to Bagardo the showman."

"Did Maldivius suffer some grave loss whilst you were with him?"

"That he did, sir. A thief made off with his scrying stone, which he called the Sibylline Sapphire. He blamed me for the loss; hence the change in my indenture."

"Who took the stone?"

"It was—let me think—Maldivius said the thief was one Farimes, whom he had known erewhile. Why, sir?"

"You'll find out when you know your new mistress, Madam Roska sar-Blixens."

"Master Noïthen, have the goodness to explain your

system of names and titles. I am but a poor, ignorant demon—"

"She's the widow of the Syndic Blixens, and now she's fain to become a Syndic on her own."

We turned into a side street and stopped before one of the larger edifices. We were admitted by a servant: a small, swarthy, hook-nosed man in the robe and head cloth of Fedirun. Presently we entered my new mistress' study, where the furnishings were as much superior to those of the chamber in Maldivius' maze, or in Bagardo's wagon, as fine wine is to ditch water. Although it was a sunny day and private citizens were not supposed to use artificial light, drawing all their illumination from the great mirror, three candles natheless glowed in a sconce on the wall.

Madam Roska sat at her desk, clad in a long robe of some sheer, filmy stuff, through which the natural Roska was plain to see. The sight of a human female in this state fascinates and excites the male, but that is just one of the oddities in the reproductive behavior of this species.

Roska was a tall, slender woman with gray hair, painstakingly done up into a graceful coiffure. She had narrow, refined features of a kind that, I was told, is deemed highly beautiful in Novaria. (I cannot judge such matters myself, since to me all Prime Planers look much alike.) Although well past her youth, she had retained much of her youthful smoothness and regularity of feature.

She smiled at us as the Fediruni ushered us in. "I see you got him, my good Noïthen."

"Your ladyship," said Noïthen, sinking to one knee and then rising again.

"Dear Noïthen, so faithful! Do show Master Zdim about my dwelling, present him to the rest of my staff, and explain his position—nay, I've changed my mind. Come hither, O Zdim."

I was flattered at being addressed as "Master," which title is not usually given to servants in Novaria. I approached.

"Are you in sooth he who served Doctor Maldivius, in his lair near Chemnis?" she asked.

"Aye, madam."

"Heard you him speak of some danger overhanging Ir?"

"Aye, mistress. He chaffered with the Syndic Jimmon over the price of revealing this peril."

"And didn't he sell your indenture in resentment of your allowing Farimes of Hendau to steal his magical gemstone?"

"Aye."

"Didst ever watch him whilst he scried?"

"As to that, madam, he insisted that I stand guard over him during his divinatory trances. So I am well acquainted with his methods."

"Ah! We shall see. Let us proceed at once to my oratory and try your knowledge. You may go, Noïthen."

Noïthen: "If your ladyship consider herself safe alone with this—this—"

"Oh, fear not for me. My little dragon-man is a model of propriety. Come, Zdim."

The oratory was a small, eight-sided room in a corner of the house, cluttered with magical paraphernalia like that of Maldivius' sanctum. On a table in the center stood a bowl holding a gem exactly like the Sibylline Sapphire.

"Is that Maldivius' gem, madam?" I asked.

She giggled. "You've guessed it. 'Twas naughty of me to let Noïthen buy it from a notorious purveyor of stolen goods, but the welfare of our land demands that it be in responsible hands. Besides, Maldivius has too many old enemies in Ir City to return hither and sue me. Now tell me just what Maldivius did when he scried!"

"Well, my lady, first he prayed. Then—"

"What prayer said he?"

"The common one to Zevatas—the one that begins: 'Father Zevatas, king of the gods, architect of the universe, lord of all, may thy name be honored forever . . .'"

"Yes, yes, I know. Then what?"

"Then he made a preparation of herbs—"

"Which herbs?"

"I know not all of them; but I think one was basil, from the smell ..."

Madam Roska got out one of her books of magic and checked through the recipes. Between this book and what I could recall of Maldivius' procedure, we reconstructed most of the spell that put Maldivius into his trances. At last we could get no further.

"Most naughty of you, Zdim darling, very naughty indeed, not to have watched more closely and remembered better!" she said, patting a yawn. I was taken aback by being addressed as "darling" and wondered if this would be repetition of my embarrassing encounter with Dulnessa the bareback rider. My tendrils, however, failed to detect any lustful emotions, and I soon learnt that this was merely Roska's usual mode of address. To get along on the Prime Plane, one must realize that human beings do not, half the time, mean what they say. She continued:

"But I do weary of this pursuit, and my art calls me. Awad!"

The Fediruni appeared, bowing.

"Take Master Zdim away," said Roska, "and put him to some simple household task until the morrow. and whilst I remember—tell Philigor to put him on the payroll at ninepence a day. Thank you."

As Awad led me away, I asked: "What is Her Ladyship's art?"

"This year, 'tis painting."

"What was it whilom?"

"Last year, 'twas making ornamental feather sprays; the year before that, playing the cithern. Next year 'twill be something else, I'll wager."

During the next few days, I learnt that Madam Roska was a very talented and energetic woman. She could never, however, adhere to any one course long enough to follow it to its outcome. She could change her mind and her plans oftener than anyone I have known, even among these fickle Prime Planers. Remembering Jimmon's words, I wondered how so light-minded a person had not only kept but even augmented the estate she had inherited. I suppose that, beneath her superficial volatility, she hid a core of hard-headed shrewdness, or else that she had had a run of astounding luck.

On the other hand, she was always poised, polite, and gracious, even to the meanest of those she commanded. When she had driven them frantic by her sudden changes of plan, and they muttered and growled against her in their quarters, someone was sure to defend her by saying:

"After all, she *is* a lady."

These gatherings of the twenty-odd servants were frequent, since Roska rode her help with a light rein. They were also hotbeds of gossip. I learnt among other things that half the unattached men of the upper classes in Ir City were suitors for Roska's hand—or at least for the Blixens' fortune. Plenty of attached ones, for that matter, would have been glad to shed the wives they had and replace them by Roska. The servants had a pool on who would succeed, but there was no sign yet that any bettor would soon collect the pot.

Between us, Roska and I reconstructed Maldivius' entire spell. We were ready to embark upon this magical work when she said:

"Ah, no, darling Zdim; I am suddenly terrified of what I might see. Here, take my place. Canst scry?"

"I know not, madam, never having tried it."

"Well, try it now. Begin with the prayer to Zevatas."

"I endeavor to give satisfaction," I said and settled myself in her chair. I recited the prayer, but without feeling, since the gods of Ning are not those of Novaria. I sniffed the fumes and spake the Mulvanian cantrip:

Jyū zormē barh tigai tyūvu . . .

Sure enough, the flickering lights in the Sapphire began to take form. First came a cloudy confusion of scenes: bits of sky and cloud, land and sea, all mixed up and shifting. One instant, I seemed to be looking down upon the earth from a height, as if I were a bird; the next, it was as if I lay on a meadow, looking out between blades of grass. Then I seemed to be sunken in the sea, where dim, finny forms moved in and out of the blue distance. After a while I learnt to control these effects, so that my viewpoint became fixed.

"What shall I look for?" I said. Speaking while in such a trance is like trying to talk with one's head wrapped in a blanket.

"The menace that Maldivius said threatens Ir," she said.

"I heard of this menace, but Maldivius did not reveal its nature."

"Think, now. Was it that some neighboring nation plans mischief?"

"I heard of no such thing. Are any of these neighbors at enmity with Ir?"

"We are at peace with all, said peace being no uneasier than usual. Tonio of Xylar is unfriendly, being leagued with Govannian against our ally Metouro; but that pot's on a low simmer for the nonce. Besides, Tonio loses his head within the year—"

"Madam! What has this man done, that you speak so casually of depriving him of his head?"

" 'Tis the custom in Xylar to cut off the king's head every five years and toss it up for grabs by way of choosing the next king. But enough of that; back to our menace. Could it be that danger threatens from some more distant land—from Shven beyond the Ellornas, perchance, or Paalua beyond the seas?"

"I remember!" I said. "Bagardo quoted Maldivius as saying that the Paaluans should make his fortune."

"Then let's fly—I mean, let your mystic vision fly— to Paalua, to see what those folk are up to."

"Whither, my lady?"

"Westward."

My vision in the Sapphire had become blurred during this colloquy, and it took another sniff of the fumes and a repetition of the cantrip to bring it back into focus. I forced my point of view to rise and moved it westward, steering by the sun. My control was still far from perfect; once I blundered into a hill, whereupon all went black until I emerged on the further side.

The hills of Ir fled beneath me, and then the coastal

plain and the valley of the Kyamos. I flashed over Chemnis with its ships, out the estuary, and over the broad blue sea.

League after league I sped, seeing nought but an occasional seabird and once a spouting whale. Then a cluster of black specks drew my regard. Soon they became a fleet. Long, sharp-ended ships they were, each with a single square sail bellying before a fair wind.

I dropped down for a closer look. The decks were thronged with figures, quite different from Novarians. Most were utterly naked, while a few had fluttering cloaks loosely thrown about them. They were nigh unto black of skin, with mops of curly hair and large curly beards. Hair and beards varied from black to rusty brown. Black eyes looked out from cavernous eye sockets under beetling brow, and their noses were wide and flat, with no bridge.

Madam Roska became more and more excited as I described what I saw. Then came an interruption. From the poop of the ship on which I was scrying came a scrawny old Paaluan, with white hair and beard. He held what looked like a human leg bone, and his eyes searched all about him. At last he seemed to stare at me from the depths of the gem. He shouted inaudibly and pointed his bone at me. The vision blurred and broke into dancing motes of light.

When I reported this to Roska, she paced the floor of the oratory, chewing her nails. "The Paaluans," she said, "are plainly bent upon bale. The Syndics must be warned."

"What do the Paaluans desire, madam?"

"To fill their larders, that's what."

"Mean you they are cannibals?"

"Exactly."

"Tell me, my lady, what sort of folk are they? I understood that, on this plane, folk who went naked and ate other human beings were deemed primitive savages. Yet the Paaluans' ships seemed well built and appointed—albeit I am no expert on such things."

"They're no savages; in fact, they have a high civilization, but vastly different from ours. Many of their customs, such as public nudity and anthropophagy, we deem barbarous. Now, what's to do? If I go to the Syndics, they'll say I do but try to alarm them in hope of getting my seat on their board. Could you bear the news?"

"Why, madam, if brought into their presence, I could tell them what I have seen. But I have no authority to demand the loan of their ears."

"I see, I see. We shall both have to do it. Summon my tiring woman."

Soon after, Madam Roska, clad for the street, called for her litter. But then a lady friend of hers sounded the door knocker. When this woman entered, there were cries of "Darling!" and "Precious!" The next I knew, the urgent mission to the Syndics was forgotten while the two women sat and gossiped. By the time the visitor left, the reflected sunlight was dimming and dinnertime approached.

" 'Tis too late to do aught today," said Roska wearily. "The morrow will suffice."

"But, madam!" I said. "If these villainous wights from across the sea be but a few days' sail from our coast, should not this news take precedence over all else? As is said on my plane, one nail in the cracked board eftsoons may save ten anon."

"Speak to me of it no more, Zdim. 'Tis a misfortune that Madam Mailakis chanced in at just that time, but I *could* not entreat her rudely."

"But—"

"Now, now, Zdim darling! The subject is highly distasteful, and I would forget the whole sorry business in the pages of a book. Fetch from the library the copy of Falmas' *Love Eternal*."

"Madam Roska!" I said. "I endeavor to give satisfaction; but—if I may speak freely—I really think you should convene your Board of Syndics forthwith. Else we may all perish, including your noble self. I should be remiss in my duties, did I not point this out to you."

"Dear Zdim! You are most thoughtful of my welfare. Awad! List the members of the Board and, after dinner, visit them. Tell them that tomorrow, at the third hour, I shall wait upon them at the Guildhall with urgent news."

At the meeting, Jimmon, the Chief Syndic, said: "Are you that demon from the Twelfth Plane that was indentured to Doctor Maldivius?"

"Aye, sir."

"What's your name? Stam or something?"

"Zdim Akh's son, sir."

"Ah, yes. Extraordinarily ugly names, you Twelfth Planers have. Well, Roska, what's this all about, eh?"

"Gentlemen," she said, "you will recall that, last month, Doctor Maldivius sought to squeeze money from the Syndicate in return for news of a peril menacing Ir."

"I remember well enough," said a Syndic. "I still think it was a bluff; that he had no such news."

"You know what a slippery character Maldivius was," said another. "No wonder they made it too hot for him to stay in the city."

"Aside from all that," said Roska, "I've learnt what the menace is, and Maldivius exaggerated not."

"Oh?" said several. They were a sleepy, bored-looking lot, most of advanced years and many fat. Now they sat up and showed signs of interest.

"Aye," continued Roska. "A powerful scry stone has lately come into my hands, and my servant has seen the menace approaching. Tell them, Zdim."

I described my vision. Some looked impressed; others scoffed: "Oh, come now, you don't expect us to take the word of an inhuman monster?"

The argument raged for an hour. At last Roska said: "Has any of Your Excellencies a talent for scrying?"

"Not I!" said Jimmon. "I wouldn't touch the stuff. Too much like witchcraft."

Others echoed the sentiment until an old Syndic, clept Kormous, said he had dabbled in the occult arts in his youth.

"Then you shall come to my house instanter," quoth Roska, "whilst Master Kormous undertakes the trance and tells you what *he* sees. Belike you'll credit him."

An hour later, Kormous sat in the chair before the Sapphire, while the other Syndics stood around. He spoke in a muffled voice, but as he did so the skins of the others paled.

"I—see—the—Paaluan—ships," he mumbled. "They are—but a few leagues—from Chemnis. They—will make land—the morrow."

One by one, the Syndics dropped their incredulity. One said: "We must posthaste back to the Guildhall, to consider our next acture."

"No time; we'll meet here," said Jimmon. "May we use your withdrawing room, Roska?"

As they filed into the room, Roska said: "At least, now you'll not deny me my seat on the Board on the frivolous ground of my sex."

"No such agreement was made ere you warned us," said Jimmon.

"Marry me, Roska darling," said a Syndic, "and you'll be a Syndic's wife, which gets you all the glory without the toil."

"Marry me," said another, "and I'll use my influence to get you your seat. 'Twould do no harm to have two Syndics in one family."

Another said: "I have a wife, but if the fair Roska would enter into an—ah—arrangement—"

"Shut thy gob, thou vulgar barbarian!" said Jimmon. "You know Madam Roska is the most virtuous woman in Ir. Besides, if she entered into any such arrangement, 'twere with me, who am much richer than you. Now, what about the black cannibals, eh?"

"If we hadn't paid Zolon to send its fleet north against the pirates of Algarth," said one, "their navy would make short work of the Paaluans."

"But we did pay," said Jimmon, "and the Zolonian navy did sail, and 'twere hopeless to try to recall them."

"It wouldn't have been, had you not taken so much time dickering with Maldivius," said another.

"A pox on you! I had to husband the taxpayers' money," said Jimmon. "Had I taken Maldivius' first offer, you'd have had my scalp for wasting the Republic's wealth. Besides, right or wrong, that's over and done with. The question is: what to do now?"

"Arm!" said one.

"You forget," said Jimmon, "that we sold our reserve stock of arms to get the money to pay the High Admiral of Zolon for the Algarthian expedition."

"Oh, gods!" said one. "What sort of mercenary idiots . . ."

And so it went for hours, with bitter recriminations. Each Syndic sought to cast the blame for the Republic's unpreparedness on one of the others. When the day was well spent, the Syndics decreed the instant mobilization of the militia and commanded all men not under arms to betake themselves to the manufacture of weapons. They appointed the youngest of the Syndics, a financier named Laroldo, commander-in-chief. Laroldo said:

"I am deeply sensible of the honor you do me, gentlemen, and I will try to merit your approval. First, however, may I suggest that we keep our proceedings secret until the morrow, at which time we shall publish our decrees and send a messenger to Chemnis to warn the Chemnites? I think Your Excellencies understand why." He winked at his fellow Syndics.

Madam Roska spoke up sharply: "Why the delay? Every hour is precious."

"Well, ahem," said Jimmon, " 'tis too late in the day to do aught useful. Besides, we would fain not excite the commons; a panic in this underground city were a dreadful thing."

"Oh, fiddlesticks!" said Roska. "I know what you're up to. You mean to scour the markets and buy up all the food and other necessities, knowing that their prices will soar—especially if Ir be besieged. Shame on you, to take advantage of the people in this heartless fashion!"

"My dear Roska," said Jimmon, "you are after all a woman, even if a beautiful and accomplished one. Therefore you don't understand these things—"

"I understand well enough! I'll tell the people of your plot to forestall and engross—"

"I think you'll do nothing of the kind," said Jimmon. "This is an executive session, with full power to control the release of its proceedings. Anyone who wantonly reveals what takes place here, before official publication, can be mulcted of his entire estate in fines. And you, my dear, are much too delicate to be a scrubwoman. Do I make myself clear, eh?"

Roska burst into tears and left the room. The Syndicate adjourned, and the Syndics gathered their cloaks and swords with unseemly haste. My tendrils told me that Roska was right; that they were frantic to get to the markets and shops ere they closed and ere rumors of the invasion sent prices up.

Next day, the orders of the Syndicate were posted, and two messengers galloped off towards Chemnis. During the entire day, Ir was in a state of furious bustle. Somewhat over four thousand militiamen—all for whom arms were to be had—and the two hundred-odd Shvenish mercenaries were mustered on the flat beyond the Tower of Ardyman. They were put through a few simple drills and marched off down the road to Chemnis. They made a brave showing with banners fluttering and Laroldo the banker, in full armor, riding at their head.

Another thousand or so remained behind on the flat, being drilled by old Segovian, the drillmaster. The youths drilled with staves and brooms until proper weapons could be found for them.

Segovian was a stout bear of a man with a grizzled beard and a voice like thunder. He was the only man in Ir who gave much thought to military matters. The other Irians looked upon him as somewhat of an uncouth, bloodthirsty barbarian. They kept him on as a necessary nuisance, like firemen and collectors of waste.

For over a century, the Republic had pursued a peaceful policy towards other Novarian nations. The Syndicate, the ruling body of the merchant aristocracy, devoted itself with single-minded acuteness to the amassing of wealth. Some of these riches were judiciously spent in hiring the navy of Zolon to ward the coast. Some went in bribes to other Novarian leaders, playing one off against another and dissuading them from combining against Ir. The policy had worked well enough with other Novarians, but the Paaluans bid fair to be focs of another kidney.

V

LAROLDO THE BANKER

DURING this day of mobilization and bustle, I remained at Roska's house to help her scry. For most of the day, however, this did us little good. The Paaluan wizards had become aware that they were being spied upon. No sooner should we get a fix with the Sapphire and their wizards would point their magical bones and spoil the picture. Therefore we had only brief glimpses of the foe.

From time to time, we shifted our view to the port of Chemnis. We kept watching and hoping for the messengers from Ir to arrive; but, as far as we could see, the town pursued its normal business undisturbed.

Late in the day, while watching Chemnis, I sighted a cluster of black specks on the western horizon. When I told Roska about them, she groaned.

"Oh, gods!" she cried. " 'Tis the man-eaters, about to descend upon the unarmed Chemnites and slaughter the lot. What delays our messengers?"

"Distance, mainly," quoth I. "Besides which, if I know you fickle Prime Planers, they're as likely as not to have stopped off at a tavern and gotten drunk. Hold! I see something else."

"What is it? What is it?"

"A man riding into Chemnis on a mule. Let me get a closer fix upon him. He appears old and bent, with long gray hair streaming out from under his hat; yet he lashes his beast to a canter. By the gods of Ning, it is my old master, the wizard Maldivius! Now I see him drawing rein as he passes a couple of Chemnites. He is shouting and waving his arms. Now he gallops on, to stop again and exhort the next passerby."

"At least the Chemnites will have received some

53

warning," said Roska. "If they believe his warning and flee at once, they may escape the stew pot."

"You Prime Planers never cease to amaze me, madam," I said. "I had opined that Doctor Maldivius was too utterly selfish to be bothered with warning anybody of doom, unless the good doctor could extract a price for his information."

"As you see, he's not an utter scoundrel. We seldom are, or utter anything else for that matter."

I continued to watch the port city. Evidently the first persons to whom Maldivius spoke disbelieved him, for they continued about their business as if nothing had happened. Little by little, however, his cries of warning began to take effect. I could see little clusters of people, standing about and gesticulating as they argued. Within an hour of the first warning, people began loading their goods into carts, or lashing them on the backs of beasts of burden, and taking the road up the Kyamos.

Less than half the townspeople had taken to the road, however, when the Paaluan fleet appeared off shore. Then terror struck. The road became jammed with hurrying townsfolk, jog-trotting and stumbling away from their city. Some went empty-handed, others with one or two treasured possessions snatched up at the last instant. I had lost track of Doctor Maldivius.

The Paaluan galleys swept into the harbor. Several drew up at unoccupied piers and quays. Paaluan soldiers dashed ashore and spread out, peering around corners as if they expected an ambush. Then whole companies disembarked, commanded by officers in feather cloaks of brilliant scarlet and yellow.

From one ship, men led down the companionway a multitude of animals unlike any I had seen. They were large creatures, big enough to carry a man in a saddle. They had slender muzzles and long ears, like those of an ass, but there the resemblance ended. They had short, clawed forelegs, hugely developed hindlegs, and long stiff tails. They progressed by hopping on their hindlegs, holding those tails up to balance the weight of their bodies. Altogether, they were something like the small Prime Plane beast called a rabbit, but on a huge scale.

As soon as the hopping beasts were ashore, the Paaluans who led them swung into the saddles on their backs and went bounding away, as swiftly as a horse can gallop. The last few Chemnites were just leaving the city, and the Paaluan cavalry caught up with some of these. Some simply rode down their victims and speared them with lances or hurled javelins into their bodies. Others whirled a device of cord and stones and threw it, so that it wrapped itself around the fugitives' legs and felled them to earth, where they were swiftly secured and dragged back to Chemnis.

It was now Madam Roska's turn to scry; but scarce had she obtained her fix when she screamed and covered her eyes. She became incoherent. To learn what had so terrified her, I had to go back into the trance myself.

Down another companionway from a ship came a procession of even more formidable creatures. The Paaluans had trained several score of their dragon-lizards as cavalry mounts. Since a full-grown dragon often exceeded fifty feet in length, one could bear several riders in tandem.

The driver bestrode the reptile's neck. Behind him came six or eight others, seated in pairs on a kind of howdah. The usual complement was four archers and two spearmen. All covered their nakedness with a curious kind of jointed armor, made (I learnt later) of pieces of lacquered leather. Although not so strong as a good suit of steel, such as Othomaean knights wear, it was light and practical. Since one galley could accommodate only a small number of these lizards, the force was divided up among many ships. Because of the limitation of docking space, it took two full days to disembark the entire force, which outnumbered ours by perhaps two to one.

Meanwhile, the Paaluans already ashore spread out and occupied the deserted buildings of Chemnis. The Chemnites whom the bouncing Paaluan cavalry had caught were slain, cut up, and prepared as food by salting or smoking.

On the third day after the landing, the Paaluan army marched up the valley of the Kyamos, with mounted scouts and flankers thrown widely out to guard against surprise.

Meanwhile, Roska's house became practically an annex of the Guildhall, the Syndics coming in at all hours for news of what we had seen. Old Kormous spent many hours in the oratory, relieving Roska and me at our scrying.

At the same time, word of the invasion swiftly spread throughout the Republic. As a result, peasantry and townsfolk stampeded from the rest of the nation into Ir City, which had the repute of impregnability. Hence the city became overcrowded, with people sleeping in the subterranean streets.

At last came the day of battle. Kormous and I were both in trance, watching the Sapphire from opposite sides of the table. We could not see much, first because of the interference of the Paaluan wizards, and secondly because of the clouds of dust.

As far as I could see, the Syndic Laroldo attempted none of those military subtleties—deceptive maneuvers and the like—that some Prime Plane nations have developed to such a pitch of artistry. He simply lined up his army, with the Shvenites around him in the center, waved his sword, and ordered them forward. Then all was lost in the dust.

It was only a fraction of an hour later, however, that we began to glimpse fugitives—Irians, not Paaluans—running madly from the battle. We saw some Irians shot or speared by the crews on the backs of the dragon-lizards, while the lizards gobbled a few. Then, as the scene shifted, I saw His Excellency Laroldo galloping eastwards. The Syndics present at this session of scrying cried aloud, beat their breasts, tore their hair, and uttered maledictions and threats against Laroldo, whom they blamed for the defeat.

The banker-turned-soldier reached Ir a few hours later and staggered into Madam Roska's home, covered with dust and blood and with several pieces of his armor dangling by single straps. He threw the stump of his broken sword on the floor and told the assembled Syndics:

"We're beaten."

"We know that, you fool," said Jimmon. "How bad is it?"

"Total, as far as I'm concerned," said Laroldo. "The militia folded up at the first shock and ran like rabbits."

"What of the Shvenites?"

"When they saw the day was lost, they formed a hollow square and marched off, presenting a hedgehog with their pikes. The enemy let them go, preferring to chase easier prey that would not fight back."

One Syndic said: "I do notice that you saved your own precious neck. A hero would have fallen trying to rally his men."

"By Franda's golden locks! I'm no hero, merely a banker. And 'twould have done you no good for me to have fallen on the field. Since we were well outnumbered, the battle would have come out the same, and you'd not have had what little help I can give you. Had I consulted my own safety merely, I should have ridden off to Metouro. After 'tis over, an we still live, you may hang, shoot, or behead me as you list. Meanwhile, let's get on with the job." My tendrils told me that the man was sincere.

"Well said," quoth another Syndic, for much of the Syndicate's rancor against Laroldo had abated in the face of so huge a catastrophe. "But tell me, Master Laroldo, we've followed your advance by the scry stone. Why tried you not some trick maneuver—a feint or a flanking movement, for example? I've read how other generals have beaten superior forces by such sleights."

"They had armies of well-trained men—veterans—whereas I had a mob of tyros. Even had I known about such maneuvers, 'twas all I could do to get my gaggle of geese lined up and all moving in the same direction at once. But now, if you crave not to be fodder for the cannibals, you needs must raise a new army. Make it of boys, grandsires, slaves, and women if need be, and arm them with brooms and bricks if swords and arrows be lacking. For those who come against us meant to salt you and ship you back to Paalua to dine on for many a moon."

"You don't suppose we could buy them off, eh?" said Jimmon. "Our treasury flourishes."

"Not a chance. Their land is mostly desert and hence poor in pasture whereon to raise edible beasts. They crave flesh, and every so often they sally forth to other continents to get it. Nor do they care whether 'tis the flesh of men or of beasts. And so, right now, one good iron arrowhead is worth more to you than its weight in refined gold."

There was a general chorus of sighs around the circle of Syndics. Jimmon said: "Ah, well, now that it's too late, 'tis easy to see the follies of our former courses. It shall be done as Master Laroldo prescribes."

"Can't we seek for aid from one or another of the Twelve Cities?" said a Syndic.

Jimmon frowned in thought. "Tonio of Xylar is hostile because of his alliance with Govannian. We shall be lucky if he try not to join forces with the invaders."

" 'Twere like one rabbit allying himself with a wolf against another rabbit," said a Syndic. "Both would end up in the wolf's gut."

"True, but try to tell King Tonio that," said Jimmon. "Govannian is hopeless for the same reason. Metouro is friendly, but their army is mobilized on the border of Govannian, to meet the threat from there. Besides which, the Faceless Five have become suspicious of their own army of late, because a revolutionary conspiracy amongst the officers has come to light. Nay, I fear no help is to be looked for thence."

"How about Solymbria?"

"Solymbria's policy of neutrality might possibly be bent—if Solymbria were not under that addlepate Gavindos."

"The gods must have meant to chastise Solymbria when they caused the lot to fall upon him," said Roska. "My bondsman Zdim were a better archon than he."

Jimmon stared at me, his eyes slits in his fat, round face. "That gives me an idea. O Zdim!"

"Aye, sir?"

"As an outlander, an indentured servant, and not even human, you are in no position to command those of this plane. Natheless, when I have heard you speak, meseemed that you made better sense than many of our wise men. What course would you suggest?"

"You ask *me*, sir?"

"Yes, yes. What would you say, eh?"

"Well, sir, I strive to give satisfaction . . ." I thought a while, during which the Syndics watched me like gamblers watching the spin of the wheel. "First of all, did I understand Master Laroldo to be a banker?"

"Aye," grunted Laroldo, who was gulping a flagon of Roska's fine wine as if it had been small beer. "None surpasses me at low interest on loans and high on deposits. Would you borrow or lend?"

"Neither, Your Excellency. But enlighten my ignorance, pray: have you in sooth had no warlike experience ere this?"

"Nay; why should I? We've been at war with no one. 'Tis usual for one Syndic to command the forces. Since I was the youngest and most active, they chose me."

"Well, sirs, on our plane, for any enterprise where the results of error be so perilous, we prefer to choose as captain a demon with practice in that line. We have a saying, that experience is the best teacher. Is there nobody in Ir who has fought with weapons?"

A Syndic said: "There's old Segovian, the drillmaster. He would have marched with the army, but we commanded him to stay in Ir and train recruits. He's no blaze of brilliance, but at least he knows which end of a spear to poke with."

"Humph," said Jimmon. "Suppose we make Segovian commander, and he raise another militia? There ought to be enough lusty farm lads amongst the refugees who've swarmed in upon us. Then the Paaluans arrive. They can't get in against even feeble resistance, so strong our position is; but neither can we break out. No matter how lavish our supplies of food and water, they'll run short in time. What then?"

"Well, sir—" I thought some more. "You say there is plenty of money in the treasury, yes?"

"Aye."

"You hired a corps of barbarians from Shven— those tall, yellow-haired fellows—did you not?"

"The bastards deserted us," growled Laroldo.

"One can't blame them overmuch," said Jimmon. "When they saw the day was lost, why should they march back hither and put their heads in the noose by reëntering the city? Go on, Zdim."

"Well then, whence came these men? I know in a general way that Shven lies beyond mountains to the north, but where exactly got you these fellows?"

"They were recruited from the Hruntings," said a Syndic.

"Where, exactly, are they?"

"The Hruntings dwell across the Ellornas from Solymbria. Their cham is Theorik, son of Gondomerik."

"If," said I, "you could get a messenger to this Theorik with a promise of much gold, could he fetch back an army large enough to vanquish the Paaluans?"

"It might be worth the trying," said a Syndic.

"Hopeless," said another. "We should do better to clear out and flee to Metouro, leaving the Paaluans to loot an empty city."

Another long wrangle arose. Some were for sending an offer to the barbarian ruler. Some protested that it would cost too much, to which the first replied that all the money in the world would do them no good when they were quietly digesting in Paaluan stomachs. Some favored a general flight; they hoped that if they could not defeat the Paaluans, they could at least outrun them.

In the midst of these wrangles, in came a militiaman, crying:

"Your Excellencies! The foe is in sight!"

"In what sort?" asked Laroldo.

"Their scouts, mounted on beasts that look like huge, long-tailed rabbits, approach the wall of Ardyman's Tower."

"Well, so much for your scheme of fleeing the city," said Jimmon. "Now must we stand, to do or die. Come on, everybody: let's view these cultured cannibals."

At the entrance to this cave-city, we found that Segovian, not waiting upon his official appointment, was already managing the defense. The main gate and the little portal above it had been closed and barred, and timbers had been propped against them to hold them shut.

We climbed the stairways up to the roof. The stouter Syndics went slowly, stopping to puff. At the top, we found a crowd of militiamen being ordered about by Segovian. He was placing one behind each merlon of the parapet with a bow, an arbalest, or a sling.

"Now hear this!" he roared. "Get your weapon ready to shoot, then pop out and discharge it through the crenel beside you. Linger not in the embrasure, lest you get a return shaft through your weasand, but duck back behind the merlon. No heroics, now; this is serious business. Pick your targets; waste not your missiles on the countryside—"

An arrow arched over the wall, to fall with a clatter on the flagstones. Segovian sighted the Syndics and bustled over.

"What are you fellows doing up here, without the least protection?" he yelled, unawed by his visitors' wealth and station. "Everyone up here is to wear a headpiece and a cuirass, though they be nought but boiled leather!"

Jimmon cleared his throat. "We have come to inform you, Master Segovian, that we have chosen you our commander-in-chief."

"Good of you, good of you," snapped Segovian. "Now off you go—"

"But pray, General!" said a Syndic. "At least let us catch a glimpse of those we fight against."

"Oh, very well; I suppose I can allow you that much," grumbled the new general. He hustled them about like an angry sheep dog, barking at them if they held their heads too long in the crenels.

Down below, a crowd of yelling Paaluan scouts

milled about on their bouncers, as we called their mounts. (The native name is something like "kangaroo.") They shot arrows from short bows, but such was the height of Ardyman's Tower that the shafts arrived with little force. Our missiles, shot from above, could have been much more effective, but our warriors' inexperience made them miss. At last a crossbow bolt struck a Paaluan, who fell from his saddle. Thereupon the rest went bouncing off to a safer distance.

A vast cloud of dust in the distance heralded the approach of the main Paaluan army. The onlookers atop Ardyman's Tower burst into cries of dismay as the dragon-lizards came in sight, swinging their limbs out and around at each stride of their lizardly, spraddle-legged gait. After them came rank upon rank of footmen, mostly pikemen and archers. They did not seem to have cross-bows, which gave us some advantage.

So began the siege of Ir. Since there was now no more question of mass flight, we had either to beat the Paaluans or perish trying. At this time I thought of the Irians and myself as "we," since my fate was linked willy-nilly with theirs.

Segovian proved a surprisingly effective general, considering the material he had to work with. Within a few days, Ardyman's Tower was defended by another five thousand militiamen, even though most were armed with improvised weapons, such as hatchets and hammers. But the forges glowed and the anvils clanged day and night, slowly building up our stock of arms. Things like iron window gratings were melted up.

In accordance with the Syndicate's policy of enlisting all slaves and bondsmen, promising them freedom after victory, I was enrolled in the artillery. Being so much stronger than the ordinary Prime Planer, I could crank the windlass of a catapult twice as fast as a pair of them, thus doubling the engine's rate of discharge.

The Paaluans set up their camp just out of bowshot of the tower. When they had it all neatly built, Segovian ordered us to open on them with our longest-ranged catapults. The darts and stone balls we sent whistling into their camp, skewering and mashing their warriors, so galled them that after a few days they struck the whole camp and moved it back out of range.

Meantime, they extended a line of earthworks around Ardyman's Tower, up Mount Ir behind the tower and down again. The hillside gave them an advantage in archery, which they were not slow to exploit. They showered us with shafts, shot from a height equal to our own, until Segovian erected a set of massive leathern awnings, like sails, along the parapet on that side to catch the arrows as they slanted down upon us. The Paaluan wizards sent illusions in the form of gigantic bats and birds swooping at our battlements, but our men learnt to ignore them.

The Syndicate sent out a messenger to go to Metouro for help. The man was lowered by a rope from the tower on a moonless night and tried to steal through the hostile lines. The next day, the sun arose to show the messenger tied to a stake in front of the camp. The Paaluans spent the day in putting the man to death with exquisite refinements.

A second messenger, commanded to try to break through to Solymbria, fared likewise. After that, it became hard to find volunteers for such missions.

The Paaluans began to build a catapult of their own, felling trees in the neighborhood for their timber. Their engine was a mighty one with a long, counterweighted boom. Segovian studied their progress through a spyglass. This was the only such instrument in Ir, since it was a new invention recently made in the far southern city of Iraz. Segovian muttered:

"Methinks I see a light-skinned fellow directing that crew. That explains how these folk, who were never known to use catapults before, can do so now. One of our Novarian engineers has gone over to them. If I ever catch the losel . . ."

I could not quite hear what it was that Segovian would do to the renegade engineer, but perhaps that was just as well. He went on:

"They're lining that thing up with our main mirror. Doubtless they seek to smash it, which would plunge our city in darkness save what light the lamps and candles can furnish. And the supply of those won't last for ay."

Luckily for us, the Paaluans—or their Novarian engineer—were not the most expert catapult builders. The first time they cranked up the device and let fly, one of the uprights holding the shaft on which the boom turned broke with a tremendous crash. Timbers from the wrecked machine flew hither and yon, slaying several Paaluans.

They began construction of a second and sturdier engine. Segovian called several hundred of his troops together and asked for volunteers to make a sortie and destroy this machine. When I was a little bashful about raising my hand, Segovian said:

"O Zdim, we need your strength and toughness of hide. You are fain to volunteer, are you not?"

"Well—" said I, but Segovian continued:

"That's fine. Have you practiced with the hand weapons of this plane?"

"Nay, sir; it has not been demanded of me—"

"Then learn. Sergeant Chavral, take Artilleryman Zdim and try him out with various weapons, to see which one suits his talents."

I went with Chavral to the courtyard of Ardyman's Tower. The courtyard had been converted to a training ground, since there was no room inside Ir for such activities. The place was crowded. One section was cordoned off for an archery range; another was used as a drill ground.

Chavral took me to the section where several thick wooden posts had been set up. The wielders of swords and axes tried their blows on these. In an adjacent space, pairs of fighters, heavily padded, fought each other with blunted weapons, while another sergeant barked commands and criticisms at them.

Chavral handed me a broadsword. "Take a good swing at yonder pell," he said, pointing to one of the posts.

"Like this, sir?" I said, and swung. The blade bit deeply into the scarred wood and broke at the hilt, leaving me staring at the hilt in my hand.

Chavral frowned. "That must have been a flawed

blade. A lot of this stuff is turned out in haste by amateur smiths. Here, try this one."

I took the second blade and swung again. Again the blade broke.

"By Astis' coynte, you know not your own strength!" cried Chavral. "We needs must find you a stouter armature." After some examination of weapons, he handed me a mace. This was a mighty club, with an iron shaft and a head that bristled with spikes.

"Now smite the pell with that ballow!" he commanded.

I did. This time the post broke, and the broken-off part bounded end over end across the drill yard.

"Now you need some practice in giving and parrying blows," he said. "Don this suit of padding, and I will do likewise."

Chavral lectured me on how to hold one's shield, how to feint, parry, circle, advance, retreat, duck, leap over a low swing, and so on.

"Now let's fight!" he said. "Two out of three knocks on the head or body win the bout."

We squared off with shields and padded clubs, weighted so that they did not much differ in heft from my iron mace. Chavral feinted and got a solid blow in against my helmet. He grinned through the bars of his helm.

"Come on, hit me!" he cried. "Art asleep? Art afraid?"

I feinted as I had seen him do and then aimed a forehand blow at his head. He got his shield up in time to catch it, but the wooden frame of the shield cracked under the blow, leaving the shield stove in. Chavral, suddenly pale, staggered back and dropped his shield.

"By Heryx's iron yard, I think you've broken my arm!" he groaned. "You there, run fetch a chirurgeon! Wine, somebody!"

He emitted a yell as the chirurgeon set his cracked bone. To me he said: "You idiot, now I shall have to fight with my arm in a sling for a month!"

I said: "I am sorry, sir; I did but strive to follow

your commands. As we demons say, to err is the common lot of sentient beings."

Chavral sighed. "I suppose I should not be wroth with you for that. But hereafter, O Zdim, methinks you had better practice by yourself, lest you lay all our warriors low with your love-taps. You need not concern yourself overmuch with the niceties of fence, for one stout blow apiece ought to do for any foeman you encounter!"

The next cloudy night, the storming party stole down the spiral ramp outside the tower. We wore soft slippers to move silently, and leathern defenses only, because of the noise of metal armor. We bore our weapons in our hands, without scabbards, lest they rattle.

Arrived at the Paaluan ditch, we tossed mattresses, confiscated from the citizens of Ir, into the ditch and had it well-nigh filled ere the foe discovered us. Then we placed a score of short ladders against their stockade and swarmed over while they were still scattered, running hither and thither and shouting the alarm.

Once over the stockade, we rushed the new catapult and piled oil-soaked fascines upon and around it. Some had brought covered buckets filled with hot coals which they now uncovered and emptied on the fascines. In a trice the thing was blazing merrily.

Meanwhile, the Paaluans rallied. Several knots of them, each led by an officer, rushed at us out of the dark. I followed Chavral's advice, confronting one cannibal after another. As each came at me, I caught his first blow or thrust on my shield and hit him a solid smack with my mace. Sometimes, but not often, a second blow was needed.

Between the feebleness of the Prime Planers and the fact that they are half blind at night, they presented no tough problem, so long as I took care that one did not come at me from the side or rear while I was engaged with another in front. I was blithely smashing skulls and staving in ribs when I heard a trumpet blow the recall. One of my fellow Irians pulled me by the arm.

"Come on, Zdim!" he shrieked over the hubbub. "You can't fight the whole army by yourself!"

I ran after the rest. At the stockade, a few Paaluans strove to keep us from recrossing. I ran down the line and smashed them one by one. Then we were running back to the tower and up the spiral stair.

When Segovian lined us up and called the roll, six or seven were missing. They told me that this was not a severe loss, considering the size of the force opposed to us; but we could ill spare any man.

The Paaluans tried to put out the fire, but the effort was hopeless. After the ashes had cooled, they began a third catapult. This time, however, they surrounded the site with a trench, a stockade, and a line of "antlers," made by whittling trec branches to many points and sinking their butts in the earth. They also mounted a heavy guard over their engine.

If none could get out of Ir, one natheless got in. The guard was aroused one dawn by pounding on the small upper portal. Looking over the battlement, they saw a stocky, hairy, naked figure, obviously not a Paaluan. They let him in and brought him before the Syndicate. I was at Roska's, preparing to go forth on my daily duty with the catapults, when a messenger came for me.

When I entered the Guildhall, a hoarse voice cried: "Zdim!" and I was hugged and pounded by my old friend, the ape-man Ungah from Bagardo's carnival.

"By all the gods of Ning, what do you here?" I asked.

"Was telling these men. When we were auctioned, yeoman named Olvis bought me. Was swinking for him when word came of the invasion. Master Olvis loaded family and self into his cart and set off for Metouro. Told me to save myself; no room in carriage.

"Set out on the same path, but along came troop of Paaluan scouts on bouncers. Ran, but not fast enough, and they caught me with whirl-balls. Threw net over me. Dragged me over stones and through mud to their camp. Would have salted me away, but their wise men had never seen a person like me. Decided to keep me alive to learn what they could."

"How got you loose?"

Ungah bared his huge yellow teeth. "Chewed my bonds. You hairless ones—not you, Zdim, but these others—have weak jaws and teeth. Strangled guard outside the tent and came away. Wasn't hard. Was brought up on hunting.

"Made one mistake. Got turned around and found self inside ring of besiegers. The camp was stirring, so I dared not try to get back out. Was telling boss men here why their spies are always caught."

"Why?"

"Smell. Paaluans have dragon-lizards trained to pick up smells. A smaller kind, and guards march about the camp with 'em on a leash, waggling long tongues they smell with." A strange look came into Ungah's face, and his little, deep-set eyes opened wide. "By Zevatas' golden whiskers, just thought of something. Remember how the dragon-lizard in the carnival loved you? I think, because you smell like reptile yourself."

"Oh, come!" I protested. "I see not why. I keep myself scrupulously clean—"

"Natheless, can smell you a dozen paces away. Novarians can't smell or else are too polite to say you stink. But you do."

"So do all Prime Planers," I said, "but I haven't complained."

"No offense," said Ungah. "Just pointed out, one creature's perfume is another's stink. Yours like lizards'."

"Well, so what? I could hardly charm all the dragons in the Paaluan army."

"No, but can wriggle through camp and away. If a lizard smelt you, he'd think you were lizard, too."

The Syndicate argued the proposal for hours. These Prime Planers are the greatest talkers in a hundred universes. Some embraced Ungah's proposal, but one protested:

"Nay; the demon owes us no loyalty. He'll abscond as soon as he gets through the besiegers. That is what I should do."

"Or," said another, "he may even go over to the foe."

"Speak for yourselves," said Jimmon. "As for his

loyalty, have you so soon forgotten the night of the raid on the catapult, when Zdim smote down more cannibals than all the rest of our party together, eh?"

"Without questioning Master Zdim's character," said another, "meseems that Master Ungah were a worthier messenger, what of his youth as a wild hunter. Besides, he's been through the camp once and knows it better than any other wight in Ir."

"We should have to make it worth his while to carry a message," said another.

"In any case," said another, "we must not shilly-shally for ay. The supply of food and water will not suffice so long as we had hoped, for the influx of refugees has put an unwonted burthen upon it . . ."

In the end, they voted to ask Madam Roska to command me to undertake a mission to Solymbria, and to ask Ungah at the same time to depart on one to Metouro. They promised him not only freedom but also a generous fee, if he and they both survived.

"I always strive to give satisfaction, gentlemen," I said. "When do we depart? Tonight? Soonest begun, soonest done, as we demons express it."

"Not quite yet," said Jimmon. "We must decide how much to offer the other Novarians and the barbarians for their help. Let's see, how many of the foe face us?"

"About seven thousand, as nearly as I can estimate," said Laroldo.

"Then we should ask a relief force of at least equal strength . . ." said another Syndic. Thus began an argument that raged for hours, touching upon such matters as the number of troops required, the proper daily pay for a mercenary, and the probable length of the campaign. Some Syndics were ever trying to trim the amount to be offered, on the ground that they must think of the prosperity of Ir after the defeat of the invaders; others, to raise it, on the ground that the money would do them no good if help could not be had.

At last a compromise was reached. I was to offer one Irian mark per man per day, plus sixpence a day for each mammoth, with a maximum of a quarter-million marks.

VI

AITHOR OF THE WOODS

THE night was as dark as the underside of a boulder—as we say in Ning—when Ungah and I were lowered in slings from the battlements of Ardyman's Tower in a drizzling rain. Segovian did not wish to open even the small upper portal, lest sound and movement draw the foe's regard. To be less visible, I turned from my normal slate-gray to black.

At the base of the tower, Ungah gave my arm a hasty squeeze and melted into the night to southward. I skulked around the tower and reached the ditch on the northern side. I sprang down into the fosse and up the far side, such a leap being nothing to a Twelfth Planer.

I paused with my ear to the stockade until I heard the tramp of a Paaluan sentry. Waiting until this sound had died away, I dug my claws into the wood of the palings and crept up and over, moving slowly like some sluggish insect.

Inside, all was quiet. The sentry had vanished. I threaded my way across the space between the inner and outer defenses, weaving between piles of equipment. The outer defenses were only a shoulder-high embankment, with enough of a ditch before it to provide the earth for the embankment.

I almost stumbled across another Paaluan sentry, sitting asleep with his back to one of the piles. With my superior night vision, I had easily seen him had I not come upon him suddenly on rounding a corner.

I could have slain him with a tap of my mace, but attached by a thong to one wrist was one of the smaller dragon-lizards used to smell out foes. As I checked myself, this reptile raised itself on all fours and shot out a long, forked tongue.

I stood as still as a statue, with my skin as black as I could make it. The lizard took a step towards me and ran the tip of its tongue up the shin of my leg. It did this several times, as if it liked me—or at least my smell.

I could not stand there until dawn, being licked by this affectionate dragon. When the creature failed to subside, I began to steal away. The dragon, however, tried to follow me. Its leash pulled on the wrist of the sleeping sentry and woke him. He stared at me and scrambled to his feet with a wild yell.

I hesitated, wondering whether to spring back and slay him or start running. I was trained in reason and logic on my own plane, but reason and logic are of small avail when one must instantly make up one's mind.

An answering shout made up my mind for me. If the alarm had already been given, it would do no good to pause to destroy this one sentry. The delay might, in fact, prove fatal to me as well.

So I sprang over the embankment, leaped the ditch, and sped north. The camp awoke with an angry buzz, as of the nests of certain stinging Prime Plane insects when disturbed. Presently, several Paaluan scouts rode forth on their bouncers, holding torches aloft. The bounding gait of these mounts caused the torches to leave fiery tracks in the dark, like the arches of a bridge across a river.

Both Prime Planers and bouncers, however, are half blind at night. With my nocturnal vision, I had little trouble in avoiding their blundering dashes. As we demons put it, well begun is half done.

The countryside north of Ir City was almost deserted. Most of the countryfolk who had not taken refuge in Ir City had fled to Metouro or to Solymbria. The few who did not get away in time had been caught and salted down for future consumption.

I ran all night and most of the next day. In my wallet I had a small map, showing the main roads between Ir and the Ellorna Mountains. In general, though, I ignored the roads and kept as straight a course to northward as I could. I reasoned that Paaluan scouts were more likely to be met on the roads than in the back-lands.

Hence I had to scramble over rocky hills, wade through swamps, and push through thickets. These probably cost me all the time I should otherwise have saved by traveling in a straight line. On the other hand, I did not meet any Paaluans.

The obstacles slowed me far less than they would have hampered one of these feeble Prime Planers, who can scarcely run up a steep hill for a few bowshots without having to halt and gasp for breath. Still, whereas we demons are stronger than Prime Planers, we cannot keep up such a pace forever. We must stop betimes, consume a substantial meal, and go into digestive torpor.

At the end of the second day, I came upon a stray sheep, which had so far eluded the Paaluan foragers. I ran the creature down and spent most of the following night devouring it. When I had finished, there was little left besides its skin and bones. I fear my act violated Hwor's injunction to obey the rules of the Prime Plane; but, as they say, necessity knows no law.

Then I took my torpor. I slept all that day, and the following night. When I awoke, I was astonished to see that the sun was lower in the east than when I went to sleep, until I realized that a day and a night had elapsed.

Not wishing to be so delayed again and still swagbellied from eating the sheep, I bethought me of other means of transport. If I could ride a horse, for instance, I could reach Solymbria City in one long ride, pausing only when necessary to rest and graze the beast. According to my map, I should soon cross the Solymbrian border.

I cast my eye over hill and dale for a horse. Sure enough, I found one, a stray like the sheep, cropping grass in a dell. It wore a bridle but no saddle.

Having seen Prime Planers ride, I had some idea of how it was done but no practical experience at equitation. On the Twelfth Plane, the animals used for carrying loads are more like those the Prime Planers call tortoises. They plod sedately along, requiring only a modicum of skill to start, guide, and stop. The Prime Plane horse is something else. But, as the saying is, we know not what we can do until we try.

I started towards this horse, slowly and quietly so as not to alarm the creature. I changed my color to match that of the grass. The horse, however, saw me coming. It rolled an apprehensive eye and trotted off.

I increased my pace, but the horse only trotted faster. I ran; the horse broke into a canter. I ran faster; the horse galloped. I slowed; the horse slowed and presently returned to its grass.

For hours that day I trailed that wretched beast without getting any closer. I bethought me that at least I ought to herd it northwards, towards my ultimate destination, so that the time should not be utterly wasted.

When the sun was low in the west, the horse at last showed signs of fatigue. It was slower in starting away as I approached. By approaching it downwind so that it should not catch my unfamiliar smell, I got close enough for a sudden dash, while its head was down feeding, and leaped upon its back. I closed my legs about its barrel as I had seen Prime Planers do, grasped two handfuls of mane, and hung on.

The instant I landed upon that horse, the creature went wild. It put its head down and began making short, stiff-legged jumps, bounding alternately to right and to left and circling. At the third jump, my grip was torn loose. I flew through the air and crashed into a shrub, with enough force to have slain a Prime Planer outright.

Freed of its rider, the horse galloped off. I dragged myself out of the bush and ran after it. By the time the sun was low, I had caught up once more with the beast, which stood with hanging head and heaving sides.

It took several stalks to get close enough to essay another leap, but I did it. This time I not only wrapped my legs about the animal's body but also clung to its neck with both arms. The horse again went into its buck-dance, but I clung with more success. That is to say, I did not lose the grip of my legs until its fifth jump. Although cast loose in that quarter, I still clung to its neck. The result was that, as I was hurled through the air, I gave its neck a terrific twist. Hence it lost its balance and fell, partly on top of me.

I clung to the animal's neck. As it made gasping efforts to breathe, I realized that my grip was shutting off its windpipe. Soon it became quiet, and I was able to seize the bridle.

Since its ribs still heaved, I knew that I had not choked the horse to death. In fact, it presently rolled to its feet and tried to back away, dragging me through dust and grass after it. I took several nasty knocks from its fore hooves, and it also bit me in the arm. At that, I slapped it hard enough to jar it.

The struggle continued until darkness fell, albeit both contestants neared the limits of their endurance. In the end, the horse was willing to stand quietly and to follow me when I led it about by its bridle. I tethered the bridle firmly to a stout, low branch of a nearby tree and lay down to rest. The horse, I thought, would also need a rest. Moreover, I did not wish to ride it at night, fearing that it would blunder over a cliff or into a slough in the dark.

The next day, I began to see signs of human life: unburnt farmsteads with smoke issuing from their chimneys, and a village or two. When I rode the horse into a village, however, the first Prime Planer to sight me let out a terrified scream.

"The cannibals! The cannibals are coming!" he shouted, running down the main street and flapping his arms like a bird about to take flight. In a trice, all the other folk were running or riding madly away in all directions. I called after them:

"Hold! Come back! Fear not! I am a messenger for the Syndicate!"

But they only ran the harder. When all had vanished, I helped myself to some food I found in a shop and rode on.

Where the road crossed the Solymbrian border, I found a customs house and, on a nearby hill, a watch tower, but both were deserted. I carried ambassadorial credentials to get me past Solymbrian soldiers and officials. I had been told to present these documents to the border post before passing on into the archonate, but there was nobody to present them to.

It took me some time to think this matter out. Should I settle down here to await the return of the missing guardians? No, I thought; Ir might fall whilst I dallied. At last I thought: hearing rumors of the invasion, the guardians may have fled to Solymbria City. The best way to carry out my orders was therefore to follow them thither. So I rode on, troubled natheless because I was not obeying my orders in an exact and literal way. On my home plane, we do not give such slipshod commands.

After crossing the border, the road to Solymbria City winds through a dense forest, mostly of ancient oaks. This woodland, called the Green Forest, is one of the few truly wild areas left in Novaria, where most of the land has been turned into farm, pasture, and city. In the Green Forest roam deer and boar, leopard and wolf and bear.

I saw none of these beasts, however. What did befall me was as follows. I was jogging along and thinking how much more sensibly we demons manage things on the Twelfth Plane, when two men stepped out of stands of dense forest on either hand, whirling ropes with large nooses on their ends.

The one on the left cast his noose at my horse's head. Seeing the circle of rope whirling towards him, the horse gave a startled leap to the right. Unprepared for such a bound, I lost my hold and flew through the air. I came down on my head on a stone.

I know not how long I lay unconscious. It seemed but a wink; but, when I strove in a dazed way to get up, more men had swarmed out of the foliage and seized my horse. When I attempted to rise, I found that they had bound my wrists behind my back and had tightened nooses around my arms and neck.

I made one effort to burst the bonds that bound my wrists, but my captors had done their work too well. Since my senses still swam from the knock I had received, I thought it better to defer attempts to flee until I learnt somewhat of my captors and their purpose. Besides, two of them kept cocked crossbows trained upon me. All were armed and roughly clad.

"Ho, by Heryx's iron yard! What's this we have caught?" said a voice. The speaker, a big man with a curly mop of brown hair and beard turning gray, spoke Novarian, but in an unfamiliar dialect.

"A Paaluan cannibal!" said one. "Slay him!"

"You are misinformed, sirs," I said. "I am no Paaluan; merely a demon in the service of the Irian Syndicate."

"A likely story!" said the man who had spoken. "Just the thing one of those ronyons would think up. We'd best slay him in any case. If he be a Paaluan, it serves him right; if he be a demon, he were no loss."

"Methinks the pilgarlic's right," said another. "Paaluans are said to be human, even if they have inhuman customs."

"Oh, shut thy gob, Nikko!" said the first speaker. "You're always gainsaying—"

"Like the nine hells I will!" cried Nikko. "When I hear nonsense, I name it as such—"

"Shut up, both of you!" roared the big, curly-haired man. "Ye, Nikko, and ye, Karmelion! If ye two brabble again, by Astis' teats I'll swinge you both! Now, methinks Nikko's right; at least, I've never heard of Paaluans' having tails and scales. Come along, O demon." He started to lead the party off into the forest. "Put another lasso on him; he may be stronger than he looks."

"More likely, he'll vanish back to his own plane and then return invisibly to murther us all," grumbled Karmelion.

They led me and my horse along a scarcely visible trail through the forest. The leader turned back to ask: "By the way, demon—"

"My name is Zdim, if you please, sir."

"Very well, then, Zdim, where did ye ever learn to ride?"

"I taught myself, the past two days."

"I might have guessed it, for seldom have I seen a

more awkward horseman. I watched you for a bowshot ere my lads snared you. Know ye not that to saw on the reins as ye do will ruin a horse's mouth?"

"Nay, good my sir; I have not had the benefit of your advice."

"Well, 'tis a marvel that ye manage as well as ye do—without a saddle, too. Ye say ye're on a mission from Ir?"

"Aye," I said, and told him of the siege. I added: "And now may I take the liberty of asking who you gentlemen are, and why you detain me?"

The big man grinned. "Ye might call us social reformers. We do take from the rich and give to the poor. As for me, you may call me Aithor."

"I see, Master Aithor," said I, realizing that I had fallen among robbers. "Taking from the rich I can understand, but on what logic do you give to the poor?"

Aithor gave a rumbling laugh. "As to that, 'tis simple. We be the poorest folk beknownst to us, so naturally we give ourselves first place in this distribution. By the time our bare necessities are met, there's never a surplus for wider charity."

"You do not surprise me, considering what I have seen of the Prime Plane. And now, what mean you to do with me?"

"That remains to be seen, good my demon. If Ir weren't under siege, we'd send a demand for ransom thither."

"What if the Syndics refused to pay?"

He grinned again. "We have ways; we have ways. Forsooth, ye shall soon see one of them."

Another hour of winding amidst the ancient oaks brought us nigh to the robbers' camp. Aithor gave a peculiar whistle, which was answered by sentries in trees. Then we marched on into the camp, which comprised a rough circle of tents and huts around a clearing. Here were twoscore more of robbers, together with a number of ragged women and children.

There was much chatter between those who had captured me and those who had stayed in the camp. Much of it I could not follow by reason of the Solymbrian dialect. I was securely tethered to a tree, to which another man was also tied. This was a stout man in rich clothing, now the worse for wear.

The man shrank away from me, being unused to one of my looks. I said: "Fear not, good my sir. I am a captive like yourself."

"You—you talk?" said the man.

"You hear me, do you not?" I told him briefly who I was and the purpose of my mission. "To whom have I the pleasure of speaking, sir?"

"At least, you have good manners for an inhuman monster," said the stout man. "I am Euryllus, a merchant of Solymbria, kidnapped from an inn in a village not far hence. Said your captors nought of my ransom?"

"Not that I heard. Should they have?"

"They set forth to meet the messenger who was to have fetched it from Solymbria, but they seem to have caught you instead. Ah, woe! If the money have not arrived, I fear for myself."

"What will they do? If they slay you, they end all chances of getting their booty."

"They have a nasty habit of sending the captive home a little piece at a time, to remind his kin and associates of his plight."

"Gods of Ning!"

"Oh, plague!" exclaimed Euryllus. "Here comes Aithor now."

The curly-haired one stood before us, massive fists on hips. "Well, sirrah," he addressed Euryllus, "your man failed to arrive, albeit we gave him two hours' leeway. Ye know what happens next."

Euryllus fell to his knees, crying: "Oh, I beseech you, good, kind captain! Give my kinsmen another day! Do not mutilate me! Do not . . ." On and on he went, weeping and babbling.

Aithor gave a sign to his men, who roughly hauled Euryllus to his feet, unleashed him, and dragged him across the clearing to a stump. They pulled off his right boot and the sock beneath it and forced his bare foot up on the stump. Then a robber smote off Euryllus' big toe with a hatchet. Euryllus shrieked.

Presently he was back at the tree with his foot

wrapped in bloody bandages. Ignoring his blubbering, Aithor said:

"Your toe shall go post-haste to your home. An we receive no reply in a sennight, some other part shall be forwarded as a reminder. When ye run short of detachable parts, we shall send your head, to show that we mean business.

"Now then, Master Zdim, ye seem to fall into a special category. Ye shall dine with me this even and tell me more of yourself and your mission."

When the time came, I was unleashed and tethered to another tree, near the hut of withes and bark that served Aithor as home. A guard stood behind me with a crossbow. Two women served us. I understood that Aithor was mate to both women, although most Novarians wed only in pairs, one man to one woman.

Aithor played the gracious host, plying me with good Solymbrian ale. My tendrils, however, picked up emanations that told me his geniality was but a veneer concealing a seething mass of hostile and violent emotions. I was by this time becoming fairly adept at interpreting the emotional radiations of Prime Planers. As the saying goes, appearances are deceptive.

Seeing no good reason to deceive him, I freely answered Aithor's questions. At length he shook his head, saying:

"I see not how to profit from your presence here. I cannot get word through the siege to your masters. If ye fail in your mission, there will be no Ir to pay ransom; if ye succeed, ye needs must be out of my grasp."

"I can promise you to ask the Syndicate to pay you after the war is won—"

"My dear demon, do I really look as simple as all that?"

"Well then, sir, what think you of my chances of success, if you release me? The Solymbrians seem to take me for a Paaluan."

"There's a muchel of ignorant wights in any land. About those tawny-haired barbarians beyond the mountains I know nought; but as far as Solymbria is concerned, your failure is as certain as the fact that water runs downhill."

"Why so?"

"Because, at the last election, the gods loaded the dice against Solymbria and gave us a government of clotpates."

"How does this election work?"

Aithor belched and slapped his paunch. "Know, demon, that we Solymbrians be a very pious folk. Centuries ago, the holy fathers determined that, since the gods manage all, the only logical way of choosing our rulers was by lot. The gods, y'see, would determine the outcome and, loving the ancient and holy polis of Solymbria, would make the lot fall to the worthiest.

"So, every year, there's a grand festival in honor of Zevatas and to our own special godlet, Immur the Compassionate. The climax is a drawing of lots. The names of an hundred Solymbrians, taken in order from the census list of citizens, are written on slips of reed paper and enclosed in nutshells. The shells are dropped into a sacred bag and shaken up. Then, before all the people, the high priest of Immur draws one nut from the bag, and he whose name is enclosed therein becomes the next year's Archon. The second name drawn becomes the First Secretary; the third becomes Censor, and so on until all the high offices of state have been filled.

"I would not be thought guilty of impiety," said Aithor with a grin, "but I must confess that the gods have sometimes made very odd choices."

"But," I said, "everyone knows that, amongst Prime Planers, some are wise and some fools—"

"Hush, Master Zdim, if ye'd not be guilty of sacrilege! For 'tis another of our sacred principles that all men are created equal and are therefore equally fitted for statecraft. The great reformer, Psoanes the Just, made this plain when he overthrew the feudal regime. For, as he argued with irrefutable logic, if some were naturally abler and more sapient than others, that were unfair to the stupid and foolish. The gods would be guilty of permitting an unjust and inequitable state of affairs to persist amongst men. But this were unthinkable, since all men know the gods to be all-wise and all-good and to intend the well-being of mankind."

"We have some pretty silly gods on my Twelfth Plane," quoth I, "but perhaps things are different in this world."

"No doubt, no doubt. Anyway, the office of Archon fell this time upon one Gavindos of Odrum, a wrestler by trade. Now that he's been in office for most of a year, the results are evident. Did ye encounter any guards at the border?"

"Nay, and that puzzled me. I had been told to expect them and had been given documents—those your men took from me—to identify myself."

Aithor: "Since none has been paid for months, they have simply deserted their posts rather than stay and starve. The rest of the Archonate is in a similar pass. Of course, such a state of affairs is not without its advantages to my merry men and me, for we need not fear soldiers and constables drawing cordons through the greenwood to entrap us. In fact, we are thinking of seizing some neighboring town and making ourselves rulers thereof. The greenwood is all very fine in summer, but in winter we long for warm hearths and solid roofs against the rain and sleet."

"Do no Solymbrians protest this condition?" I asked.

"Oh, aye, there's some grumbling. Some say the gods chose Gavindos to punish Solymbria for the sins of its people."

"What sins?"

Aithor shrugged. "To me, they have been no more sinful of late than men are everywhere and everywhen; but that's what is said in explication. Others say that, even if Gavindos and his helpers be fools, 'tis only fair to give the stupid a chance at the government, lest the clever exploit them without mercy and without end."

"I thought you said no Solymbrians believed that some men were stupider than others?"

"Nay, messire demon, that's not what I said. Psoanes taught that all men are *created* equal, but that the differences in their subsequent lives modified them, so that some ended up wiser than others. The cure, then, were to assure everyone an upbringing of the same degree of benignity. But this, none of our rulers have been able to effect. Parents differ at the outset and therefore impose differences upon their offspring."

"Meseems the only alternative were to rear all infants in public institutions, then?"

"One archon tried that, years ago; but the scheme aroused such opposition that the next archon rescinded the plan. In any event, the contingencies of chance perpetually disturb the pattern, raising one and casting down another without regard to his merits." Aithor scratched, doubtless being plagued by the parasitic insects of this world. "I must own to a certain skepticism about this official theory, since my brother and I, brought up in the same way by the same parents, have turned out as different as fish and fowl. He's a minor priest of Immur, as correct as a mathematical diagram; whereas I—I am Aithor of the Woods . . ."

The garrulous chieftain rambled on about anecdotes in his own career to illustrate the points he had made. When I got a chance to speak, I said:

"Master Aithor, if your government be of no avail to us of Ir, you have several score of lusty rogues here, who might be made into a formidable force of soldiery."

Aithor guffawed. "Be ye proposing to enlist *us* in your campaign?"

"Aye, sir."

"Nay, nay; no governmental employment for us, thank you! Besides, an we put ourselves in the hands of officials, they'd use us to raise your siege and then hang the lot of us when we were no longer useful. I've known such things to happen."

"You were speaking of seizing a town and making yourself its government."

"That's different. Were I lord of a town and its environs, recognized as such by my peers in government, I might feel differently. But such is not now the case."

"If the Paaluans capture Ir, the next place they'll invade is Solymbria. Its present weakness invites attack, does it not?"

Aithor: "Well, and so what?"

"They'd overrun your Green Forest and flush you out."

"I think not. We know this greenwood like the palms of our hands. They're desert folk, from what I hear, and 'twere child's play to mislead and entrap them amidst our wildwood."

"Would you not help to save the rest of your native land from devastation? Meseems that love of one's country is one of the few emotions that persuades Prime Planers betimes to put the general good ahead of their own advantage."

"Why should we? Half of us would perish in the struggle, and—as I've reminded you—the rest would be slain afterward on trumped-up charges. No, thank you. Others may risk their hides for their native land, even though she have ground them down and cast them out; but not Aithor of the Woods."

"But think! If Solymbria be devastated, what will be left for your band to prey upon?"

He chuckled. "O most sapient argufier! By Astis' pretty pink teats, Master Zdim, ye should have been a professor in the Academy of Othomae. Well, I'll tell you. We have amongst our booty a muchel of fair raiment, more suited to the person of an ambassador than a naked, scaly hide. Since it is of little use to us here, I'll accouter you properly for your mission and dispatch you on the morrow. How's that?"

"Very fine, sir—"

An outburst of yelling interrupted me. Two robbers—the same Nikko and Karmelion who had quarreled before—were going for each other with knives. Aithor leaped to his feet with a blazing oath and strode across the clearing. The chieftain's demeanor had changed alarmingly. He roared like a lion, and the veins in his temples stood out in the firelight.

He seized the two disputants, one with each hand. Nikko he hurled into a cooking fire; Karmelion he slammed into a tree trunk with such force as to stun the man. When Nikko bounded out of the fire, scattering coals and beating at the burning spots on his garments, Aithor felled him with a buffet.

"By Heryx's iron yard!" he thundered. "I warned you varlets. Lash them to trees!"

When this had been done, Aithor took a heavy whip and, roaring and cursing, flogged these men's bare backs until their flesh hung in bloody shreds. Whenever he fetched a particularly loud shriek from one, he answered it with a bellowing laugh. He ceased only when both men had swooned and even his mighty arm faltered with fatigue.

When he came back to where I was tethered, he shouted for more ale. I began a question: "Sir, if I may be permitted—"

But Aithor bellowed: "Get out, lizard-man! Count yourself lucky that I visit not the same treatment on you. Get back to your proper tree and pester me not!"

VII

GAVINDOS THE ARCHON

NEXT morn, Aithor was genial once more. He returned my belongings—all but the money—and gave me a fur-collared robe and a velvet cap to match. The cap they had to fasten on with a strap, since my skull is ill-suited to Prime Plane headgear. Then Aithor led me to a saddled horse and gave me instructions for managing the creature.

"That is not my horse," I said.

"Nay; 'tis an older beast we had here, whose decorous gait were better suited to your horsemanship. Your former steed is too good to let you ruin it by inexpert handling. Besides, ye'll now have the comfort and security of a saddle."

Fearing that Aithor might, in one of his playful moments, have my tail or some other member cut off, I forbore to argue the point. I was compelled, however, to say:

"But good my sir, whilst I might manage with that horse, I can hardly cover the distance hence to Shven without any money at all, to buy food and lodging for myself and fodder for my beast."

"Ye mean ye demons buy things with money, like a human being?"

"On the Prime Plane, I needs must do as the Prime Planers do. If you send me forth destitute, my journey will abort ere well begun."

"Ye can borrow from taverners on the credit of the Syndicate."

"O Aithor, from the way Solymbrians scream and run at the sight of me, I anticipate enough trouble even to gain admission to inns. Were you a taverner, would you give me credit?"

Aithor chewed his beard. "I see what ye mean. Well then, steal a lamb or a fowl and dine on it."

"And have the countryside up and hunting me? Come, come, Captain Aithor. You know better."

"Oh, the nine hells with it. I'll give you enough to take you to Shven, if ye be careful. Ye should get there in a sennight, and three marks a day should be ample therefore." He counted out twenty-one marks and dropped them into my wallet. "How ye fare after ye shall have reached the steppe is your problem, and wherret me no more about it."

My tendrils told me that one of Aithor's rages was brewing not far beneath the surface, so I did not "wherret" him further. A couple of robbers led me back to the road and dismissed me.

The gait of that swaybacked old nag certainly proved sedate. It took a mort of beating with a switch I cut from a branch to get the creature from a walk up to a trot, and never did I persuade it to canter more than three lopes at a time.

Withal, I reached Solymbria City on the evening of that same day. I rode in through an unguarded gate. The streets were deserted. When I halted the horse and leaned over to ask a passerby the way to an inn, the man stared at me for a trice, then put his fingers in his mouth and whistled.

Two other men ran out of a tumbledown house, and

all three attacked me. One tried to pull me out of the saddle by one leg, while the other two strove to reach me with knives. I grasped my mace, which hung by its lanyard from my saddle, and crushed the skulls of two attackers with one blow each. The third man fled into the night.

I looked around for some officer to whom to explain the two corpses but saw none. So I left them lying and rode on until I passed an inn, which I recognized by the skull of an ox above its door.

This door was bolted, and it took much knocking and shouting to get the taverner to open it a crack. When he glimpsed my face, he gave a cry of terror and tried to shut it again, but I got my foot into a crack.

"I am a cash customer!" I cried. "A guest! An envoy from Ir!"

By much repetition and argument, I prevailed upon the man to admit me, even if he stood nervously with an iron-bound cudgel poised while I showed him my documents. When I had made arrangements for lodging, I told the taverner of my encounter of that evening.

"No wonder, if you ride the streets of Solymbria after dark!" said he, whose name was Rhuys. "The place swarms with brigands."

"Is nought done to abate this nuisance?"

"Practically speaking, no. The constables, being unpaid and undisciplined, have oft turned robber themselves. Others have hired out to citizens as private bodyguards."

"A strange land and a strange city," I said. "Has it always been thus?"

"Nay; last year 'twas a fine, orderly place. But under that ninny Gavindos, pox take him, all's gone to pot. Ah, well, an we can survive another month, there will be another election. Belike the gods will give us an abler archon."

Despite my protests, it took me two days to get an audience with the archon. In the meantime the taverner Rhuys, finding that I was not quite the monster I looked, became friendly. I was his only current guest, business having become ruinously bad. When, on the day after my arrival, he set forth to buy provisions, he urged me to come with him.

"Nobody would be such a dunce as to attack me in your company," he said.

"What are those?" I pointed to a gaggle of women being shepherded along the street by a pair of burly men-at-arms.

"Housewives on their way to market," he explained. "The armed men are former constables whom the householders of one block have hired as guards. They've arranged for all the women of the block to market in concert, so that the guards can go with them to ward them from rape and robbery."

"You Prime Planers are strange creatures," I said.

"How so? Do you better in demon land?"

"On the Twelfth Plane, a demon properly reared by his parents adheres to decent behavior thereafter without constant compulsion. Hence we have little of this raveled and oppressive machinery of laws and coercion that obtains here. But you human beings—the instant you are freed from constraints, you run wild like insensate beasts, abusing and preying upon one another, like—like—"

"Like crabs in a bucket," said Rhuys.

"Thank you, sir; I could not recall the name of those scuttling aquatic creatures."

"We're not all thieves and murderers at heart," quotha. "In fact, most of us do be peaceable and orderly, asking only to be let alone to earn our livings."

"But enough of you are of the other kind, if I may say so," I said.

"Rhuys sighed. "I fear me you are right. Do no demons ever misbehave?"

"Oh, certes; but the fraction is small enough to be easily mastered. Besides, our wizards have puissant spells, which compel one accused of crime to speak the exact truth. This greatly simplifies the task of ascertaining the culprit's guilt."

Rhuys looked sharply at me. "Does the Twelfth Plane permit immigration?"

"I misdoubt the question has hitherto come up.

When I return thither, I will try to learn and let you know."

When at last I was ushered into the palace, I found Gavindos of Odrum a short man with a barrel-shaped body and very long, muscular arms. He reminded me of my friend Ungah, the ape-man.

"Siddown," he said. "What said you your name was?"

"Zdim, Your Excellency."

"Stim, Za-dim—oh, the nine hells with it. I'll call you 'Hey, you.' Have some beer. What you here for?"

"I am an envoy from Ir . . ." and I explained the circumstances of my visit.

"Ir. Let's see. That's some futtering foreign country, isn't it?" As the man spoke, my tendrils picked up emotions of bewilderment, as a child might feel when these high matters were explained to it.

"It is the republic adjoining yours on the south, sir."

Gavindos: "I always get them futtering foreign places mixed up. So, what's that got to do with me?"

"The Syndicate of Ir urgently requests that you, sir, dispatch an armed force to break the siege of Ir City."

"Huh? You mean they want my futtering army to go down and fight these clowns from—what did you say the futtering invaders are called?"

"Paaluans, sir. They come from across the Western Ocean—"

"All right, all right. I heard you the first time. Have some more beer. So why should I send my futtering army to this place—Ir, be that it?"

"Aye, sir."

"And send my futtering army across the ocean to fight these clowns in some place I never heard of— what was I saying?"

I explained again. Gavindos wrinkled his brow. At last he said:

"But look here, if the people of Ir have tails and scales like you, I don't want no futtering part of them. If these other clowns kill them and eat them, I say good riddance."

"But, sir, as I have tried to explain, the Irians are

just as human as you are. I am merely a demon bound
to their service."

"Then if they be human, why didn't they send a futtering human being to me?"

"Because I was the only one who could get through
the Paaluan lines."

The archon took a mighty swallow of beer, "Let's
see, now. Be those clowns from over the sea attacking
Ir, or be Ir attacking them?"

I explained once again.

"Well," said Gavindos, "I don't see what good it
would do me to interfere. We don't seem to have no
futtering money to pay our futtering army where it be,
let alone sending it into foreign countries I never heard
of."

"Your Excellency! When the Paaluans have cleaned
out Ir, they'll invade Solymbria next."

"Huh? You think they might?"

"Certes!"

"Which of 'em be likely to invade? Ir or—I've forgotten the futtering name of the other?"

I explained again. The archon pondered. At last he
said:

"Well, let 'em come. I'll challenge their head man
to a wrastle! I'll break his futtering back, and they'll
have to go home because they won't have no general
no more to give 'em orders. Have some more beer before you go."

VIII

YUROG THE SHAMAN

LIKE the southern part of Solymbria, the northern was
infested by robbers. I suspect that some of the rough-
looking men I saw on the road or in inns were of this
type. Some gave me hard looks, but none molested me.

I suppose my appearance dissuaded them from any nefarious plans they may have entertained.

On the second day after leaving Solymbria City, I came to the foothills of the Ellorna Mountains. While eating my supper, I showed the taverner, one Hadrubar, my map and asked him about the road across the mountains.

"Hard to tell," said he. "The Needle's Eye"—he pointed to the place on my map that showed the pass over the crest of the range—"is closed in winter by snow. Now it's high summer, and the pass should have been open for two months or more. But nary a traveler has come through from the land of the Hruntings."

"How about travelers northward bound?"

"Some have set out hence, but none has returned. Some say the Zaperazh have closed the pass."

"The what have closed the pass?"

"The Zaperazh—you know, the tribe of cave-men that dwell thereabouts. It used to take a regular military campaign every year to open the pass against their opposition. Then the government made a treaty with 'em, but with murthering savages like that, one never knows."

"What are these cave-men like?"

"Would you see one? Step hither."

He led me to his kitchen. There a surly-looking, tawny-haired youth, with a thin iron collar of a slave around his neck, was washing dishes.

"That's Glob, my Zaperazh slave," said Hadrubar. "An ill-natured scrowle, almost more trouble to train and discipline than he's worth."

"Are cave-men enslaved as a regular thing?"

"No more, since the treaty."

"This treaty did not, evidently, restore to Master Glob his liberty."

"Of course not! Some such silly proposal was mooted when the treaty was being higgled; but it roused such a towrow among Solymbrians who've paid good money for slaves that the archon rejected it. After all, unjustly to rape us of our property were a tyranny no man of spirit would submit to."

As he led me back into the common room,

Hadrubar continued in a lower tone, so that Glob should not overhear: "Under previous archons, the border was so well patrolled that runaways had little chance of slipping across; but now . . ."

"As we say in demon land," quoth I, "it is an ill tide that washes nobody's feet clean."

Hadrubar shot me a sour look. "Waste not your sympathies on those brutes, who esteem not the niceties of civilization even when they're forced upon 'em."

"This is not my world, Master Hadrubar, and it is no concern of mine how you Prime Planers entreat one another. I am, however, often puzzled by the gap between your professed principles and your actions. For ensample, you contemn Glob's primitive folk; yet methought Solymbrians believed all men to be created equal?"

"You have it wrong, sir demon. That Immur created all Solymbrians equal is a plain fact, attested by divine revelation. Who made the other peoples of the world, and how, I know not. The Zaperazh have a god of their own, hight Rostroi. Belike this Rostroi made the Zaperazh; if so, he botched the job."

I forbore to carry the argument further, thinking it illogical to dogmatize about these Zaperazh without having known any personally.

Novaria has excellent roads linking the capitals of the cleven mainland city-states. (The twelfth, Zolon, is on an isle in the Western Ocean, off the Solymbrian coast.) The road north from Solymbria City, however, was less well kept. After it crossed the border of the polis—where I passed another deserted customs house—it dwindled to a mere track, suitable for pack animals but hardly passable to wheeled vehicles. In the steeper places, freshets had washed the dirt off the bare bones of the mountains. My poor old horse slipped and stumbled so on the rocks that I had to dismount and lead him, scrambling from ledge to ledge.

By the end of the first day out of Hadrubar's Inn, I had left the border leagues behind and begun to climb. All the next three days I climbed, while the snowy ridges ahead loomed closer and closer. In the foothills rose dense stands of trees with dark-green needles, looking almost black. As I got higher, these forests thinned out to a mere scattering.

As Hadrubar had implied, there was no traffic. The silence was broken only by the sigh of the wind, the purl of a torrent, and the echo of my horse's hooves from a cliff. I sighted distant flocks of wild goats and sheep, and once a bear on a far hillside frightened the horse.

The increasing cold made me sluggish and stiff. The robe that Aithor had given me was of little help, since we demons do not have a source of internal heat like the higher animals of the Prime Plane. Hence our bodies cool down to the temperature of the ambient air, and our activity slows proportionately. The first two nights, I could thaw myself out enough by my campfire to carry me through the following day; but then I found that I needs must stop at midday, build a fire, and warm myself then as well.

On the fifth day after leaving the inn, I reached the pass called the Needle's Eye. The track wound up and down fearsome precipices. Snow lay in isolated banks and patches. Huge, snow-clad peaks towered to right and left.

At noon by my pocket sun-ring, I stopped to build a fire. The horse ate a small bagful of grain that I carried for such emergencies, since there was too little herbage at this height to keep him fed.

Gathering material for a fire proved onerous, for there was nothing to burn save a few gnarled and scattered shrubs. Moreover, between the cold and the thinness of the air, I had become so sluggish that I could scarcely move. After an hour of burdensome efforts, I collected enough combustibles. Moving like one of those Prime Plane garden pests called snails, I kindled my fire.

I hardly had the blaze going when a strange thing happened. My tendrils detected magic. Then, with a roar, a blast of ice-cold air swept down upon me. It seemed to come from overhead. It flattened out my little fire, which blazed up fiercely and then died almost as quickly as the twigs were consumed.

I lurched to my feet, meaning to put more fuel on the fire. By the time I had stood up, however, the cold had so slowed my movements that I became as rigid as a statue. Not being well braced, I toppled slowly over—fortunately not into the dying fire—and lay stiffly in the posture I had reached when I lost the power of movement.

The horse pricked its ears, snorted, and began to shamble away, clop-clop. Then came a snapping of bowstrings and a whistle of arrows. The horse screamed, reared, and fell over thrashing as several shafts struck it in the side. Others, missing their target, clattered and tinkled against the rocks. One fell near me, and I saw that the arrowhead looked like glass.

Later, I learnt that this was indeed the case. The cave-men of the Ellornas are in the stone age of culture. Discovering that glass was as easily worked as flint and furnished even sharper edges, they had made a practice of trading furs with the Solymbrians for the cullet from broken bottles and windowpanes. This they wrought into arrowheads and other tools and weapons.

The archers now appeared from behind boulders and streamed down into the path. Some began cutting up my dead horse with knives of flint and glass. Others clustered around me.

The Zaperazh looked at first sight like some sort of bear-men, but as they got closer I saw that this was the result of the furs wherein they were clad from head to boots. They were evidently of the same species as the Novarians and other human Prime Planers, not members of another species as in the case of Ungah. They were taller and heavier on the average than the Novarians. From what I could see of their faces past the fur hoods, beards, and dirt, they were not ill-looking men as Prime Planers go, with hair of assorted hues and eyes of brown or gray. Their smell, however, was overpowering. Frozen stiff as I was, I could do nought to avoid it.

They yammered in their own tongue, being even greater chatterboxes than the Novarians. I did not, naturally, understand a word of their speech. There seemed to be two leaders among them: a very tall,

middle-aged man, and a stooped, white-bearded oldster. The former ordered the tribesmen about but
paused betimes to consult in an undertone with the latter.

They turned me over and unfastened my robe to ex-
amine me in detail, with much pointing of fingers and a
perfect torrent of words. At last four of them picked
me up, one by each limb, and bore me off. The rest
followed laden with masses of flesh from the horse, of
whom little was now left but the skeleton.

I could see little of the route we followed, since I
was in a supine position and could neither turn my
head nor roll my eyes. I could only stare at the sky,
with my pupils closed down to slits against the glare of
the sun.

The Zaperazh dwelt in a village of leathern tents,
clustered about the entrance to a huge cave at the base
of a cliff. They bore me through the village, which
swarmed with women and young, and into the cave.
The darkness of the cave was soon banished by torches
and by a multitude of little stone lamps, which they set
around the floor at the edges. Each lamp was a shallow
dish with a handle to one side, and in it a wick in the
form of a lump of moss, floating in a pool of melted
fat.

To the rear of the cave, dimly illumined, stood a
stone statue, twice the size of a man. It appeared to
have been sculptured from a big stalagmite. It had
holes for eyes and mouth, a knob for a nose, and a
male organ as big as any of its roughhewn limbs.

For a while, the Zaperazh ignored me. There was an
infinity of coming and going and of ceaseless talk.

What with the village fires at the entrance, the lamps
and torches, and the swarm of Zaperazh, the cave was
warmer than the air outside. I began to thaw out. I
found that I could move my eyes, then my head, and
lastly my fingers and toes.

While I was still planning how best to use my new-
found mobility, the white-haired oldster whom I had
seen before came through the milling mass and stood

over me, holding a lamp and peering. Presently he leaned over, grasped my hand, and gave a sharp tug.

I ought to have pretended to be rigid still, but the move caught me by surprise. I jerked my hand away from the Zaperazh, betraying the fact that I was recovering my normal lissomness. The old man shouted to some of his fellow tribesmen, who hastened up. Some wrenched off the robe and the cap that Aithor had given me; others bound my wrists and ankles together with rawhide thongs. Those who had taken the garments amused themselves by trying them on, roaring with laughter at each other's appearance thus garbed.

The oldster set down his lamp and seated himself cross-legged beside me. He asked me a question in a language I did not know. I could only stare. Then he said in broken Novarian:

"You speaking Novarian?"

"Aye, sir."

"Who you?"

"My name is Zdim. Whom have I the honor to address?"

"Me Yurog, shaman—what you call wizard—of Zaperazh. But *what* you? You not man."

"Nay, sir, I am no man. I am a demon from the Twelfth Plane, on an errand for the Syndicate of Ir. May I take the liberty of inquiring your purpose?"

Yurog chuckled. "Demons evil, wicked things. But you got nice manner, anyway. We sacrificing you to Rostroi." He nodded to the idol at the back of the cave. "Then Rostroi send us many sheep, many goats to eat."

I tried to explain the reason for my journey and the urgency of my mission, but he only laughed off my explanations.

"All demons liars," he said. "Everybody know that. We no fear your black men, even if they true."

I asked: "Doctor Yurog, tell me, pray. I was told that a treaty between your folk and the Solymbrians provided for the safe passage of travelers through the Needle's Eye. So why should you seize me?"

"Treaty no good! Solymbrians promise give us one ox every month, to eat, so we let people through pass.

When Gavindos become chief of Solymbrians, he no sending oxes no more. He no keep treaty, we no keep him either. All flatlanders liars."

"Did you capture me by a magical spell that froze me stiff?"

"Why, sure. Me great wizard. Not know freeze spell make you hard like stone, like snake or lizard from flatlands. That make it easy for us, ha ha."

"Well now, behold. You have cut up my horse for food and leather, and it must have almost as much meat as one of those oxen the Solymbrians used to send you. Wouldn't you consider that a fair payment of toll to allow me to pass on through your land?"

"No great treaty with you. You enemy. All flatlanders enemies; all demons enemies. Is right to sacrifice them whenever we catching them. Tell you what, though. Zaperazh like me to skin you, slowly; but, because you nice demon with good manner and because of horse, I cut your throat quick-quick, so you got hardly no pain. Is good of me, yes?"

"Aye, though it were better still to treat me as a friend—"

Before I could carry this interesting discussion further, the tall chief loomed up and spoke to Yurog in his own tongue. Yurog replied and added in his atrocious Novarian:

"Chief, must meet guest. Is demon Zdim. Zdim, meet Vilsk, chief of Zaperazh. I got nice manner, too, yes?"

Then the chief and the shaman went off together. For some hours I had nothing to do but lie in my bonds and watch the cave-men prepare for a grand festival. The first item was to be a ceremony in honor of Rostroi, to be followed by a feast on the remains of my horse, washed down with some sort of beer they brewed and kept in leathern bags.

The sun was setting when the Zaperazh gathered in semicircular rows at the entrance to the cave. The men occupied the foremost rows, with women and children in the rear. Many of the women were nourishing their infants by means of those protruding lacteal glands that distinguish the females of the higher animals of the Prime Plane. The stench of the crowd was overwhelming. My tendrils picked up emotions of intense anticipation.

One tribesman sat down beside the statue of Rostroi with a drum, while another, with a wooden pipe of the flute kind, sat down on the other side of the idol. Vilsk made a speech. It went on and on and on. He gestured, shook his fists, stamped, shouted, roared, growled, whispered, laughed, wept, sobbed, and went through the entire gamut of human emotions.

Because of the crowd, I could not tell from my tendrils how sincere Vilsk was in his histrionics. But the tribe took the oratory with the utmost relish. This can be understood from the cave-men's lack of urban amusements.

Vilsk finished at last, and the musicians struck up. A squad of dancers, stripped to breechclouts and weirdly painted and befeathered, went into action, leaping and prancing. The dancers shouted continuously to one another, I suppose exhorting one another to get in step and to be ready for the next figure in the dance.

I seemed to have been forgotten for the moment. Having now fully thawed, I tested my bonds. These were by no means so secure as those that Aithor's men had put upon me, for the Zaperazh had assumed that my strength was no greater than that of a man. While the eyes of the audience were fixed upon the bounding, whirling, stamping dancers, I put forth my full strength and broke the thong holding my wrists. Waiting a moment for circulation to return to the members, I then grasped the thong around my ankles and snapped it, also.

Then I began levering myself slowly along the ground, a few digits at a time, towards the entrance to the cave. In the dim light, none observed as I slithered around behind one horn of the crescent formation in which the Zaperazh sat.

When I thought it safe, I rolled over and got to my hands and knees. I had almost reached the exit when a child saw me and set up an outcry. A woman turned at the sound and screamed.

Before any could lay hand upon me, I bounded to my feet and ran out the entrance. Behind me, the cave seemed to boil as the entire tribe scrambled up to pursue me.

I sped out the cave and through the tent village. As I passed a fire, near which a pile of flesh from my horse was stacked, I had the wit to snatch a steak from the pile before speeding off into the night.

Had the ambient air been warm, I should have easily escaped from the Zaperazh. My strength and my night vision gave me an advantage over Prime Planers that was usually insuperable. The cold of this height, however, soon slowed me down to no more than a Prime Planer's speed.

Behind me, a swarm of cave-men ran in pursuit, setting up a view halloo as my scales reflected the light of their torches. I bounded down the rocky slope, swerving to right and left in an effort to shake them off. But they were fast and hardy as human beings go. The swarm of torches, like a flight of luminous insects, came bobbing after me no matter which way I ran. In fact, they gained upon me. With every stride, I slowed as the cold took hold of me.

Had I known the terrain better, I could doubtless have given them the slip by some ruse; but I did not. Closer and closer they came. If I turned at bay, I could slay two or three, but then I should learn what it was like to be slowly hacked to death by crude weapons of stone and glass. And this, I was sure, would not at all give satisfaction to Madam Roska and the Syndicate, which I was obligated to do.

An arrow whistled past me. Desperation at last spurred my sluggish wits.

Making sure that they saw me, I changed color to the palest shade I could—a pearly gray. Then I angled off to the right. When they were pelting after me and yelling in anticipation of an easy triumph, I leaped down a bank that stood athwart our path. As I vanished momentarily from the sight of my pursuers, I changed my color to black and ran along the foot of the bank to the left, perpendicular to my former direction.

In a trice, the mob of Zaperazh poured down the bank and went on in the direction they had been running. I trotted lightly off in my new direction, taking care not to spurn stones and make a clatter. By the time the tribe discovered that their pale-gray quarry was no longer in sight and came to a halt, shouting and waving their torches, I was beyond their grasp.

By dawn, I had found the footpath through the Needle's Eye and was on my way down the northern slopes of the Ellornas towards the steppes of Shven.

During my captivity and flight, I had been inclined to agree with the taverner Hadrubar's unfavorable view of the Zaperazh. As I walked down the trail in the rosy light of dawn, taking a bite now and then from the slab of horsemeat, I achieved a more rational view. The Zaperazh had merely acted in the normal manner of Prime Planers, who instinctively divide up into mutually hostile groups. Each member of such a group regards all other groups as not fully human and therefore as fair game or legitimate prey. These divisions can be formed on any pretext—race, nation, tribe, class, belief, or any other difference that will serve.

Having, as they thought, a grievance against the Solymbrians, the Zaperazh had, by the normal workings of the human mind, taken a hostile attitude towards all Novarians. Since I was working for a Novarian government, they placed me in the same category. The fact was not that the Zaperazh were "murthering savages" in distinction to the civilized Novarians, but that all human beings had a touch of "murthering savage" about them, however they disguised it by a veneer of civilized manners and custom.

IX

CHAM THEORIK

FOR three days I plodded over the flat, grassy, wind-swept steppes of western Shven without seeing a sign of human life. In fact, I saw no animal life, even, save birds and a few antelope and wild ass far off. I had long since finished the horsemeat and had no means of getting more food, since the wild animals were too swift even for me to run down and I had no missile weapon.

Lacking food and water, I was weakening when my tendrils picked up a hint of dampness. I stood at gaze, testing the air, and set off in the direction indicated. In half an hour I found a water hole, surrounded by a few small trees. The water was largely mud, but I did not let that stop me. Luckily, we demons are proof against nearly all the diseases of the Prime Plane.

I was still sucking up muddy water when the sound of hooves aroused me. As I arose, the horseman spurred his beast to a gallop. He was a big man, similar to the Shvenite mercenaries whom I had seen at Ir. He wore a bulbous fur hat, a sheepskin coat, and baggy woollen trousers tucked into felt boots. His blond beard blew in the wind.

I held up my hand and cried in Shvenish: "Take me to your leader!" This was one of several phrases that I had memorized before setting forth. Time and a good instructor had been lacking for a complete course in the language.

The horseman shouted something like *"Yipi!"* and continued his charge. As he came, he unfastened a coil of rope that hung from his saddle and whirled a noose on the end about his head.

Evidently, the man intended to snare me with his

lariat, as Aithor's robbers had done in the Green Forest, and drag me along the ground. Not relishing such treatment, I braced myself. As the loop came whirling towards me, I sprang into the air and caught the rope in my claws. As I came down, I dug in my heels and threw myself backwards.

The results were astonishing. The rider was prepared to pull me off my feet and drag me, but the unexpected tug from my end jerked him out of the saddle, to fall on his head in the grass. The horse halted and fell to grazing.

I hastened to the fallen man. When I turned him over, I was still more astonished to find him dead. The fall had broken his neck.

This put a new complexion on things. The man's garments would furnish me with some insulation against extremes of temperature, for the midday heat of the steppe nearly prostrated me and the cold of midnight froze me almost to immobility. I therefore adopted the man's fur hat, sheepskin coat, and felt boots. The trousers I gave up because of the discomfort of cramming my tail into them. I also adopted the man's weapons and his flint and steel.

The horse I essayed to catch. Repelled by my looks and odor, it moved away as I approached. At the same time, it seemed reluctant to leave the neighborhood of the water hole. I pursued it round and round the clump of trees in a circle; but, weak from hunger, I could not catch it.

Then I bethought me of the lariat. I had never practiced the art of casting nooses, and the first time I tried it I only wound the rope around my legs and sent myself sprawling. Several hours of practice, however, enabled me to make a fairly good cast up to twenty feet. By this means I succeeded at last in getting close enough to throw the noose over the horse's head. Then I led it back to the water hole and tethered it to a tree.

The dead man I ate, rejoicing in being able to cook my repast for a change. Some Prime Planers would be horrified and deem me a mortal enemy of mankind, but I cannot take their illogical and inconsistent tabus seriously. The man had brought about his own death by attacking me. His soul had presumably gone to that Prime Plane afterworld, where everything is done by machinery. If he had no more use for his body, I certainly did.

Knowing men's peculiar feelings about the devouring of their own kind, however, I buried the dead man's remains. It would be hard enough to engage these barbarians in a rational discourse without giving them an additional reason for hostility.

Then I mounted the horse and steered it northwest. According to the map I had once possessed, this was the way to Cham Theorik's horde. One could never be sure, because every few sennights the tribe packed up and moved in search of new grass for their flocks and herds.

On the second day from the water hole, I sighted another rider on my left. He was headed in a more northerly direction than I, so that our courses converged. Like the first nomad, he wore a fur hat and a sheepskin coat.

As the man and I neared each other, I waved. Here, I thought, was he who should show me to the horde's present encampment.

The man waved back, and I thought I had made a friendly contact. When we drew nigher, I called in my rudimentary Shvenish:

"Sir, would you please direct me to the camp of Cham Théorik?"

We were now about twenty or thirty paces apart. Evidently the man was near-sighted, for only now did he appear to notice that the face under the fur hat was not that of a fellow tribesman after all. His eyes widened with horror, and he shouted something like: "Aroint thee, vile demon!" He pulled the bow from his bow case and fumbled with the arrows in his quiver.

I had a bow and a quiver, too, but never having practiced archery I had no hope of hitting him before he skewered me. Moreover, I wanted a guide, not another corpse.

My next actions were quite out of character. Had I stopped to plan them rationally, I am sure that I should have abandoned the scheme as rash and foredoomed. I had never even practiced the maneuver, which were difficult at best. But as we demons say, luck often befalls the fearless.

I jabbed my horse's flanks with the sharp corners of the heavy iron stirrups, which the Shvenites employ in lieu of spurs. As the beast bounded ahead, I swerved towards the mounted Shvenite. While the latter was still nocking his arrow, I swooped within a few feet of him. Then, doing as I had seen Madam Dulnessa do in Bagardo's circus, I threw myself up on my hands, gripping the saddle bow, and brought my feet up under me. In a trice I was standing erect on the back of the galloping horse.

If I had had to go any distance, I had surely fallen off this precarious perch. By this time, however, the two horses were almost in contact. I sprang from the saddle on which I stood to the rump of the other horse and slipped into the riding position just behind the other rider. I grasped his neck with both hands, driving the ends of my talons into his throat beneath his beard, and shouted in his ear:

"Take me to your leader!"

"I will take you!" he cried in a strangled voice. "Only pray cease digging your claws into my neck, lest you open my veins and slay me!"

I let him continue on his course. The poor fellow did not realize that I was as weak with terror at my own recent daring as he was at my unfamiliar aspect.

The movable city of the Hruntings reminded me of the camp of the Paaluans and even of the village of the Zaperazh. The houses, however, differed from either of these, being made of sheets of felt spread on hemispherical frameworks of poles. Around this mass of gray domes, areas were marked off for special purposes, among which I noted horse lines, an archery range, and a park for war mammoths.

The nomads and their females and young swarmed about the mass of felt tents, among which were also placed hundreds of large four-wheeled wagons. As my captive guided his mount through the spaces between these obstacles, he and the other nomads kept up a running fire of shouts. My man cried:

"Keep off! Stand back! Interfere not, or this thing will slay me!"

In the midst of the tent city stood a tent of double size, with a clear space around it. Before it rose a pair of standards bedight with horsetails, human skulls, and other emblems of nomadic sovranty. A pair of Hruntings, in cuirasses of lacquered leather, stood guard before the cham's tent; or rather, were supposed to be standing guard. One sat with his back to one of the standards and his head bowed on his knees, asleep. The other sat with his back to the other standard; while not asleep, he was idly spinning a little wooden top with thumb and forefinger on the hard soil before him.

At my captive's shout, both sentries hastily rose. After an exchange of words with my captive, the sentry with the top clumped into the tent and soon returned to say that the cham would see me forthwith.

I leaped down from the horse and walked towards the entrance. My captive also dismounted and started for me, drawing his sword and yelling threats. I half drew my own blade, but at this point the sentries intervened. They pushed him back with the shafts of their spears; I left them shouting, and entered.

Part of the oversized tent had been partitioned off as an audience room. As I came in, the cham and two more guards scrambled into official positions and assumed expressions of dignified sternness. The cham sat on a saddle placed on a block of wood to hold it clear of the floor, thus giving visitors the impression of the fearless leader of intrepid horsemen. A guard in fancy dress, with squares of gilded brass sewn to his leathern cuirass, stood on each side of the cham with spear and shield.

Cham Theorik was an elderly Hrunting, as tall as I and hugely fat, with an enormous white beard curling down his chest. He wore a purple robe embroidered with silken patterns from far Iraz. Golden hoops, chains, and other gauds larded his neck and arms.

As instructed, I got down on all fours and touched

my forehead to the carpet, remaining in that ungraceful pose until the cham said: "Rise! Who are you and what do you want?"

"If," I said, "Your Terribility could furnish an interpreter of Novarian, since I know little Shvenish—"

"We speak Novarian, also, our good—we cannot say 'our good man,' now can we? Ho ho ho!" Theorik slapped his sides and guffawed. "In fact, we are told we speak it perfectly. So we will proceed in that tongue."

Actually, the cham spoke Novarian with such a thick accent that I could not understand it much better than I could his Shvenish. I did not, however, deem it prudent to offer my opinion. I related the circumstances of my visit to Shven.

"So," said Theorik when I had finished, "the money-grubbing Syndicate wants us to save them from the fruit of their own avarice and poltroonery, eh? Or so you say. Where are your credentials, and where is the Syndicate's offer in writing?"

"As I have told Your Terribility, the cave-men of the Ellornas took all my papers when they captured me."

"Then what proof have you?" He wagged a fat forefinger. "We have a short way with people who try to deceive us. They are apt to find themselves with sharp stakes up their arses, ho ho ho!"

By a mighty effort of thought, I found a solution to this latest snag. "Great Cham, before the invasion, a few hundred Hruntings served Ir as mercenaries. After the battle, these men marched off to their homeland. Some will remember seeing me in Ir."

"This shall be looked into. *Rodovek!*"

"Aye, sire?" said an official-looking Hrunting, issuing from a curtained doorway.

"See that Master Zdim be lodged in a style proper to an ambassador. See also that he be guarded against attack from without—or against escape from within. If he turn out in sooth to be an ambassador, well and good; if not, ho ho ho! Now then, Master Zdim, you shall return hither at sunset, when our chieftains and we hold a drunken tribal council. We shall then discuss your proposal."

"Excuse me, sire, but did I hear you say 'drunken tribal council'?"

"Certes. Know that it is our custom to discuss all at two councils, the first drunken so that thoughts shall come freely and fearlessly, the second sober so that reason and prudence shall prevail. The sober council will be on the morrow. Fare you well, lizard-man; you have our leave to go."

My last glimpse of Cham Theorik on this occasion showed his two guards, with much heaving and grunting, getting him off the saddle he used as a throne.

The drunken council was held in a pavilion in the open space behind the cham's abode. Unlike the latter, it was a tent of canvas, supported by poles and guys like the main tent of Bagardo's circus. In fact, it had a familiar look. It harbored fifty-odd chiefs and other tribal officials, stinking worse than the Zaperazh.

When I had been shown my place, my table mate on one side was an extremely tall, powerful young Hrunting, with shiny hair the color of gold falling to his shoulders. He was Prince Hvaednir, a nephew of the cham. Since he belonged to the same royal clan as Theorik and was the strongest and handsomest man of that clan, he was considered next in line for the rule of the Hruntings. As he spoke only a few words of Novarian, he and I exchanged no more than polite amenities.

The neighbor on the other side, Prince Shnorri, was short and fat. He, too, belonged to the royal clan. More to the point, he was fluent in Novarian, having studied at the Academy at Othomae. To him I spoke of the familiar look of the tent.

"It is no wonder," said Shnorri. "An I mistake not, this is the same tent that your circus man employed. When his properties were auctioned, an enterprising trader brought it over the Ellornas and sold it to the cham. He argued that it would hold more diners with less weight and bulk than would one of our traditional round tents of poles and felt.

"The deal caused a great to-do amongst the Hruntings. Some said: Buy the tent, for it represents progress. Progress is inevitable, and our only defense against it is to keep up with it. Others said: Nay, the old and tried ways are best. Besides, to use essentials from Novaria were to make ourselves dependent upon the Novarians, who would soon, by greed and trickery, reduce us all to beggars. As you see, the party of progress prevailed."

The council began with a dinner. Unlike the Novarians, the Shvenites chewed loudly with their mouths open. The huge drinking jacks were set out and filled with beer by the women. The cham and his chiefs began guzzling.

The time arrived for toasts. The Shvenish custom differs from the Novarian. Novarians drink to others whom they would honor; the honored one remains seated and abstains while his dinner mates rise and drink to him simultaneously. A Shvenite, on the other hand, stands up, boasts of his prowess, and drinks to himself. For ensample, one burly fellow with a broken nose stood up, belched, and declaimed as fellows:

"Who has led the foremost in every battle? I, the fearless and invincible Shragen! Who slew five Gendings single-handed at the battle of the Ummel? I, the mighty and valorous Shragen! Who won the inter-clan wrestling tournament in the fifth year of Cham Theorik, on whom may the gods ever smile? I, the fierce and redoubtable Shragen! Whose sense of honor has never failed him? Mine, that of the noble and virtuous Shragen! Can any warrior compare with the peerless and well-beloved Shragen? Nay, and therefore I drink to my own magnificence!"

Down went a mugful of beer. When the magnificent Shragen had sat down, another arose and delivered a similar harangue, which Shnorri translated for me. As we say at home, self-conceit oft precedes a downfall.

After an hour of this, the chiefs of the Hruntings were well into their cups. At last, Cham Theorik hammered on his table with the hilt of his dagger.

"Time for business!" he bellowed. "We have two

items only tonight. One is a complaint from the Gendings that one of our brave heroes has stolen a flock of their sheep. The other is the proposal brought from Ir by the demon Zdim—that dragonny-looking fellow yonder, between Shnorri and Hvaednir. First, the sheep. Step forward, Master Minthar!"

The Gending envoy was a middle-aged Shvenite, who told how a Gending had been robbed of fifty sheep by a gang of Hrunting thieves. Cham Theorik questioned Minthar. No, the victim had not seen the rustlers. How knew he they were Hruntings? By his shepherd's description of their costume and horse trappings, and by the direction in which they had fled . . .

After an hour of this, during which several chiefs went to sleep, Theorik ended the proceedings. "Enough!" he roared. "You have produced no competent evidence. If the Gendings need more sheep, they can buy them from us."

"But, Your Terribility, this is a weighty matter to us—" protested the envoy.

Theorik belched. "Begone, wretch! We do not believe a word of your tale. Everybody knows what liars the Gendings are—"

"Everyone knows what thieves the Hruntings are, you mean!" shouted the envoy. "This means another war!"

"You insult and threaten us in our own tent?" yelled Theorik. "Guards, seize me this pestilent knave! Off with his head!"

Guards dragged Minthar, screaming and struggling, out of the tent. A buzz of argument arose among the chiefs. Several tried to speak to the cham at once. Some said that this was the way to treat those treacherous scum; others, that the person of an ambassador should be respected regardless of his message. By shouting louder than the other, one of the latter party got the cham's ear.

"Aye, aye, we see your point," said Theorik. "Well, we will consider the matter again on the morrow, when we are sober. If Minthar merit a more considerate treatment—"

"Cham!" cried my companion Shnorri. "Minthar

will be in no state tomorrow to get better treatment!"

Theorik shook his head in a puzzled way. "Aye, now that you put it thus, I see what you mean. Guards! Belay our last order, about killing—oh oh, too late!"

A guard had just stepped into the tent, holding at arm's length, by its scalp lock, the dripping head of Ambassador Minthar. Theorik said:

"A good joke on us, ho ho ho! By Greipnek's balls, we shall have to think up some excuse or apology to Cham Vandomar. The other item is the proposal brought from Ir by the demon Zdim . . ."

Theorik gave a résumé of my proposal. "At first we suspected some sessor trick," said the cham, "for Zdim brought no credentials or other evidence with him, claiming they had been stolen by the Zaperazh. Several of our men who served in Ir, however, confirm that Zdim was there, in service to a lady of that city. So we are inclined to believe him. At least, it is hard to see what ulterior motive he could have in making so long and arduous a journey by himself. But now let him speak to you in person. His Excellency Zdim!"

By "sessor," Theorik meant a non-nomad, like a farmer or a city-dweller. The nomads use the word as a term of contempt for all men of sedentary occupations.

I had some difficulty in standing up, for Prince Hvaednir had fallen asleep with his golden head on my shoulder. When I had disengaged myself from him, I told the chiefs of the facts, while Shnorri translated. I was circumspect in my speech, having seen what might befall an ambassador who roiled this crowd of drunken barbarians.

The ensuing discussion ran on and on. Because the speakers were now thoroughly drunk, their arguments were also largely irrelevant or unintelligible. At last the cham rapped for order.

"That will be all for tonight, comrades," he said. "We shall come to our deshish—our deshiss—we shall make up our minds tomorrow at the sober council. Now—"

"I crave your pardon, Great Cham, but it is not all!" cried a Hrunting, whom I recognized as the man I had forced to convey me to the tent city. "I was fain not to interrupt your business; but now that is over, I have something to settle with this demon!"

"Oh?" said the cham. "What would you, Master Hlindung?"

"He has insulted my honor!" Hlindung told of our meeting on the steppe and of my coercing him to bear me to the cham's abode. "So I name him a vile, inhuman monster and will prove my words upon his corrupt and loathsome body, forthwith! Stand forth, demon!"

"What means this?" I asked Shnorri.

"It means you must fight him to the death."

"Cham!" I called. "If this man slay me, how shall I present the proposals from Ir on the morrow?"

"Let that fret you not," said Theorik. "I have heard the proposals, and I am sure that Shnorri as well knows them by heart. Meanwhile, this combat will provide an amusing end to a prolixious evening. How jolly, ho ho ho! Stand forth and take your chances, Master Zdim!"

Hlindung swaggered back and forth in the space before the cham's table. He bore a sword, which he swished through the air, and an iron-studded leathern buckler.

"I endeavor to give satisfaction," I said, "but what am I supposed to fight him with?"

"Whatever you have with you," said the cham.

"But I have nought with me!" I protested. "Your guards disarmed me when they took me into custody, and my weapons have never been returned."

"Ho ho ho, how funny!" roared Theorik. "How unfortunate for you! I cannot order that you be given weapons, for you might hurt Hlindung with them, and then I should have been disloyal to my own tribesman. Come on, push him out, somebody."

My tendrils tingled with the lust of the assembled chiefs to see blood flow. Hvaednir awoke, and he and another seized me by the shoulders from behind and began to push me out from behind the table.

"What if I kill him?" I cried to the cham.

"That would be a fine jest, ho ho ho! Why, nought so far as I am concerned, since you would have slain him in fair fight. Of course, his kinsmen would then be at feud with you and entitled to slay you on sight."

Before I knew it, I stood in the cleared space, facing Hlindung. The latter went into a crouch, holding his shield up before him, and began to slink towards me, making tentative little motions with his sword, on whose blade the yellow lantern light danced.

"But, Your Terribility—" I began, when Hlindung rushed.

Although in strength I far surpassed the ordinary Prime Planer and was more solidly put together, I did not delude myself that Hlindung's sword would simply bounce off my scales. Since the space was cramped, I did the only thing I could to avoid that wicked-looking blade. I leaped clear over Hlindung's head, alighting behind him.

The Hrunting was well gone in drink, whereas I had drunk only a moderate amount of beer. Besides, alcohol seems to affect us of the Twelfth Plane much less than Prime Planers. Perhaps the alchemists can puzzle out the reason.

When Hlindung realized that I had vanished, instead of turning around, he slashed the air where I had been standing. "Witchcraft!" he shouted. "Demonry!"

I sprang upon him from behind, seizing the collar of his jacket and the slack of his trousers with my talons. Then I swung him off his feet and spun him in a circle, wheeling on my heels. The third time around, I let him go on the upswing. With a scream, he flew against the sloping side of the tent and went right on through. A thump came from outside.

Several Hruntings rushed out. Presently some came back in, saying:

"Great Cham, Hlindung is not badly hurt. He merely broke a leg coming down."

"Ho ho ho!" chortled the cham. "So my brave swasher thinks he can take liberties with beings from other planes, eh? This will teach him. He should be harmless for a few moons. By the time he recovers and can seek a return match, Master Zdim, you will doubtless have found business elsewhere. Cursed clever of you, by Greipnek's bowels! Even if you did damage my tent. To bed, everybody; I pronounce this drunken council ended."

The sober council, the following afternoon, was less picturesque but more reasonable, despite the hangovers of some of the chiefs. In fact, some Shvenites displayed reasoning powers that would not shame a Twelfth Plane demon. The chiefs favored an expedition to Ir but boggled at the dragon-lizards.

"The mammoth is a fell weapon," said one, "but the beasts have a craven mislike of wounds and death. Confront them with some outlandish sight and smell, like these dragons, and they are wont to panic and flee back through their own host. This leaves the host in an untidy state."

"We demons," I said, "have a saying: to seek to save oneself is a natural law. But have you no magicians amongst you, to render these monsters harmless?"

"We have a couple of old warlocks, good only for curing bellyaches and forecasting the weather. We brave nomads had rather trust our sword arms than the juggleries of magic."

"If the Paaluans invaded Shven," mused another, "it were simple. Wait for a cold spell, and their dragons—being cold-blooded reptiles—would slow to a halt as the cold stiffened them."

"That gives me an idea, if I may take the liberty of speaking," said I. "I know a shaman of the Zaperazh—if 'know' be the word I want for a man who tried to sacrifice me to their god. He has a cold spell in his magical armory; in fact, they captured me when this fellow Yurog froze me so that I could not move. Now, could we persuade Master Yurog to apply his spell to the Paaluans . . ."

This suggestion met with shouts of approval from the chiefs. "Good!" said the cham. "That is, *if* Master Zdim can enlist this savage in the enterprise. We'll march as far as the Needle's Eye and then see what his powers of persuasion will do.

"Now," he continued, "another matter. We still have no written contract with the Syndicate, and we should be fools to bleed ourselves white on their behalf without a solid agreement. We know those tricksters all too well. We could sacrifice half the nation for them, but if we had no piece of parchment to show, they would say: 'We owe you nought; we never agreed to your helping us.' "

There was general agreement with the cham. Since nearly all Shvenites are illiterate, they have a superstitious reverence for the written word. Besides, from what I had seen of the Syndicate, I doubted not that the Shvenites' apprehensions of being cozened had a basis in fact.

In the end it was decided that, first, an expeditionary force of five thousand warriors and a hundred mammoths should be sent as far as the Needle's Eye. If I could enlist Yurog, the force would then march on through Solymbria, which would be in no position to resist the trespass, to Ir.

After some chaffering, they and I agreed upon essentially the terms the Syndicate had offered: one mark per man per day, with sixpence a day for each mammoth and a maximum of a quarter-million marks. They insisted on adding a minimum of a hundred thousand marks, to which I acceded.

Before engaging the Paaluans, however, we should make every effort to get a written promise from the Irians. How this could be done, with Ir surrounded by the Paaluans, would have to wait upon the event. Lastly, Theorik said:

"O Hvaednir, since you may some day succeed me, it is time you learnt the art of independent command. Therefore you shall lead this foray. I shall furnish you with a competent council of war, made up of seasoned commanders, and I advise you to heed their rede."

"I thank you, Uncle," said Prince Hvaednir.

X

GENERAL ULOLA

WE marched to the Needle's Eye. Our scouts caught a Zaperazh tribesman, told him that we wished to confer with Yurog the shaman, and let him go. Presently, Yurog appeared from among the rocks. A payment of ten oxen to the tribe—five at once and five promised after the campaign—easily persuaded him to join us. As we swayed down the southern side of the pass on the back of a mammoth, the old fellow confided:

"Is nice, being shaman; but me want see civilization, meet great wizards, learn higher magic. After many years, rocky mountains and ignorant cave-men is big bore."

At the Solymbrian border, we faced the problem of how to treat the Solymbrians. I told Shnorri:

"Methinks they cannot stop your army on its march to Ir, since they have become disorganized by having a halfwit as archon. But they will soon hold another election, and this time the lot may fall upon somebody more competent. If Hvaednir let his men run wild, robbing, raping, and slaying, you may have to fight your way back through Solymbria after the campaign."

At the next council of war, Shnorri brought up the subject. (I attended these councils as the representative of Ir.) A chief said:

"Who is this faintheart, who would have us treat vile sessors in this delicate, namby-pamby fashion? Out upon him! If our brave lads futter the Solymbrian wenches, it is a favor to the Solymbrians, by infusing our heroic blood into their degenerate veins."

"Even a rat will bite if cornered," said another. "Therefore, I agree with Prince Shnorri. If we push these Solymbrian rats too far, they will surely retaliate.

114

What boots it for us to slay ten of them for every one of us? That one man who would die is worth far more to us back on the steppe, if war with the Gendings flare up again."

"Oh, bugger the Solymbrians!" said the first. "We shall go through them like a hot knife through butter. Have you forgotten how we sacked Boaktis City in the days of Cham Yngnal, whilst the sessors fled like rabbits before us?"

Shnorri said: "I also recall that, as our force was on its way back across the Ellornas, the combined forces of the Boaktians, Tarxians, and Solymbrians assailed us and recovered most of the loot."

So it went, back and forth, while Prince Hvaednir listened. This young man did not strike me as very intelligent, even when I had learnt enough Shvenish to converse with him. Thus far, however, he had listened attentively to the advice of his chiefs and accepted it when they more or less agreed. At last he said:

"I will follow my cousin Shnorri's advice. Command the warriors to stay on the highway; straggling shall be severely punished. Moreover, they shall pay the price demanded for everything they take from the Solymbrians. Theft and assault shall be punished by the loss of a hand; rape, by castration; murder, by the loss of a head."

There was grumbling at this, and some warriors seemed not to take the command seriously. After one had lost his head for manslaying, however, the rest settled down and obeyed the rules.

At first the Solymbrians fled wildly from the Hrunting army. When they learnt how well-behaved the nomads were, however, most returned to their domiciles. A host of sutlers, entertainers, and whores assembled to minister to the warriors' wants.

From some of these, I learnt that Ir still stood. The news was not new, because all the land roundabout Ir City, for many leagues, was bare of human life. Some of the folk had been captured by foraging parties of Paaluan kangaroo-cavalry and taken back to be eaten. The other dwellers, hearing of the fate of their countrymen, had put all the distance they could between themselves and Ir.

When we marched past Solymbria City—which prudently closed its gates against us—we passed a camp of Irian refugees. We halted for the night in sight of the city, and a delegation of Irians waited upon our commander.

"We fain would join your army in the rescue of our city," they said. Shnorri again translated.

When Hvaednir seemed at a loss as to how to take this offer, Shnorri suggested calling a council of war. This was done. One chief asked:

"How many would you be?"

"Perhaps five hundred, sir."

"How are you armed?" asked another.

"Oh, we have no arms, sir. We fled in too great haste. We thought that your well-stocked army could furnish the arms."

"How many are seasoned warriors?" asked a third.

The spokesman began to look depressed. "None, sir. We are a peace-loving folk, who ask only to be allowed to till our farms and ply our trades." A Hrunting made a sneering remark in his own tongue, but the Irian continued: "Natheless, we burn with patriotic fervor, which makes up for our lack of experience."

A chief said: "I fear that, with such a covey of fumblers, one might carry out one good charge but hardly a campaign. How are you mounted?"

"Not at all, sir. True, a few brought horses; but these are mere hackneys and farm nags, unsuited to war. We meant to serve as foot soldiers."

Hvaednir spoke up: "We are a completely mounted army. Every man, save the mammoth riders, has at least two horses. What use would a battalion of untrained infantry be to us? You could not even keep up with us on the road."

Several chiefs remarked: "A plague on them! We need no crowd of cowardly sessors." "Aye, they would only be in the way." "Honor demands that we keep the glory of this campaign to ourselves." "Send the lowns packing, Prince."

The Irians could not understand, but they caught the

tone and looked sadder than ever. As they prepared to depart, I said:

"Sirs, you know not what you will find at Ir. The Paaluans may have thrown strong defenses around their position. For assailing these, if I read my Prime Plane history aright, your animals will be of no use. You would have to undertake a siege of your own, which is a slow, laborious business.

"Whilst you made your preparations, the Irian refugees could catch up with you. If you lent them a Novarian-speaking officer as drillmaster, he could train them on the road. When the time came to assault a fortified camp, you might find that one soldier afoot is much like another."

There was another outburst from the chiefs. Most of them still objected to arming the Irians, although Shnorri and two others came over to my side. At length Hvaednir said:

"Well, since the arguments are balanced, let us let the gods decide."

He took a coin out of his purse, flipped it, caught it, and slapped it down on his wrist.

"Heads," he said. "The Irians shall be armed and mustered as the demon proposes. I have spoken."

The weather became hot as, marching through deserted country, we neared Ir. The Hruntings' heavy garments were unsuited to this sultry climate. Men rode with heads and upper bodies bare and then complained of sunburn. (Most Shvenites shaved the scalp save for a braid scalp lock; Hvaednir, vain of his golden locks, was one of the few to wear a full head of hair.) The stout Shnorri suffered especially, the sweat cascading off his rotund body. Sickness became common.

I must say that, when it came to moving an army, throwing out scouts, or pitching and striking a camp, the Hruntings were efficient. The chiefs might be full of fantastic notions of honor, valor, and superiority, but in practical matters they were effective. Hence it did not much matter that Prince Hvaednir was a rather stupid young man. So long as he followed their advice, he could not go very far wrong.

As we neared the Kyamos, our scouts reported that the Paaluans still surrounded Ir City. The Kyamos itself could not be seen from Ir, because of a low ridge between the Kyamos and the little Vomantikon. It was therefore decided to march by stealth and at night to the Kyamos and camp there, in hope that the Paaluans would not discover our presence until we were ready to attack. The cannibals no longer sent their scouts out on bouncers to range the countryside. I suppose they had given up searching for anything—or rather, anybody—edible, and it had not occurred to them to watch for a relieving army.

One evening, the Hrunting army moved quietly into the valley of the Kyamos, crossed the drawbridge, and camped. The men ate a cold supper, and all would have gone well had not one of the mammoths uttered a shrill, trumpetlike squeal. Several others responded, and within minutes our scouts reported that a body of Paaluans on bouncers were issuing from their camp with torches. The chiefs dispatched a larger force of horsemen to deal with them. The Hruntings scattered the Paaluans and killed most of them, but some got back into the camp.

The cannibals now knew that there was a hostile force nearby, but they did not know what sort of force it was. The chiefs strove to keep them from finding out. They posted pickets along the ridge separating the Kyamos from Ir and sent horsemen to patrol the higher points in the area, day and night. Some Paaluan scouts may have glimpsed our camp, but from too far away to do them much good.

On the second night after our arrival, the war council convened. A chief reported:

"Our scouts tell me that the Paaluan soldiers were busy around their camp all day with picks and shovels, enlarging their fortifications. Some dig pits and plant stakes at the bottom; some set up barricades of sharpened branches; some dig ditches and raise walls. We should attack at once, ere these savages make themselves impregnable."

"Nay!" said another. "We are the world's most dashing horsemen; but stumbling about afoot, we should get ourselves slaughtered to no end. Better to cut off their supplies and starve them out."

"We should starve the Irians to death whilst we were about it," said another.

"So what? When the craven sessors are all dead, we can help ourselves to their wealth."

"That were dishonorable counsel!"

"Comrades!" said another. "Let us keep our minds on the present problem. The Irian foot are but a day's march behind us. If we await their arrival, we shall be better able to storm the cannibal camp. We shall, of course, put the Irians in the first wave. After all, it is their city, so they should not mind dying for it."

And so it went, round and round. At last Prince Hvaednir remarked:

"Comrades, my uncle the cham warned me, ere we departed, against joining battle without a firm agreement on terms with the Syndicate."

"But how shall we agree with the Syndicate," said a chief, "with the circle of Paaluans betwixt us and them?"

"We could go over, under, or through," said a chief, half in jest. "From the amount of barc rock hereabouts, I doubt if a tunnel were practical."

"As for going over," said another, "have we no magician who can fly an envoy into and out of the city? I have heard of enchanted rugs and broomsticks that could carry a man."

Shnorri said: "When I was a student at Othomae, a lecturer told me that such spells had been cast. But only the mightiest wizards could cast them, and they only with costly preparations, long labor, and the exhaustion of their own strength and powers. We might, however, ask our own magicker, Yurog the Zaperazh."

Yurog was fetched. When the proposal was explained to him, he sighed. "Me no great magician like that. Me just little tribal shaman. Me hope learn stronger magic in civilized countries, but no have chance yet."

Shnorri: "My friend Zdim here, I understand, es-

caped from Ir through the Paaluan lines by stealth and
by his power of changing color. If he did it once, why
not again?"

"Gentlemen, I endeavor to give satisfaction. I must,
however, point out that the task were harder and
riskier than before. As we say on the Twelfth Plane,
every pitcher goes to the well once too often and gets
broken. The Paaluans are raising stronger defenses—"

The chiefs drowned me out. "Hurrah for Zdim!"
"Zdim shall be our trusted messenger!" "With those
claws, he can go over a stockade like a squirrel." "You
are too modest, noble Zdim; we will take no denial!"

The council was unanimous. I cast a look at Prince
Hvaednir, hoping he would gainsay them; the lad had
been showing more independence lately. But he said:

"You are right, comrades. Zdim shall take a contract
into the city, get the Syndics' signatures, and fetch it
out again. Until he do so, we shall remain here and
merely harass the cannibals. I have spoken."

Since I saw no other way to serve Ir as commanded,
I accepted the mission, albeit with reluctance. Writing
materials were brought. The learned Shnorri inscribed,
both in Shvenish and in Novarian, in duplicate, a contract between the army of the Hruntings and the Syndicate of Ir. The terms were those agreed upon at the
Hruntings' camp in Shven: one mark a man a day and
so on. Shnorri and I signed. Hvaednir made his mark,
which Shnorri and I witnessed.

Ere the moon arose, I neared the Paaluan camp.
The earthworks on which the besiegers had been laboring presented no great obstacle, because only a fraction
had yet been completed. I threaded my way on all
fours across the band of broken earth and half-finished
works to the main ditch and embankment.

Again I crept into the ring-shaped camp, with my
hide a midnight black. I watched, listened, and sniffed
for sentries and their ban-lizards. If I say so myself, I
moved as quietly as a shadow.

I was halfway across the space between the inner
and outer walls and was circling a pile of logs, when I
sensed the approach of a sentry. I froze against the

logs. Around the corner he came, with a lizard trotting beside him on a leash. He walked past without seeing me.

But his lizard felt my presence. The reptile stopped and thrust out a tongue. Feeling the tug on his leash, the Paaluan halted and turned to me. As he took a step back, his hand brushed against my scales.

The man jerked his hand away, stared into the darkness, and leaped from me with a yell. As other shouts answered him, I started to run, dodging around obstacles towards the inner wall. In rounding a bend, however, I cut the corner too closely. I tripped over a tent rope and fell sprawling, half bringing down the tent.

I was up again instantly, but in that instant a man appeared with a torch. As I started to run again, something hummed through the air and wrapped itself around my legs, bringing me down once more. It was one of those devices of stone balls whirling on the ends of a cord.

Before I could untangle myself, it seemed as if half the Paaluan army had pounced upon me. Two or three I could have handled, but these fellows clustered about and hung on to my limbs like a swarm of those Prime Plane insects called ants. I bit one in the leg, but that did not stop them from binding my arms and legs with enough rope to have restrained a mammoth.

They even roped my jaws together so that I could not open them. Then they bore me to an inclosure and tossed me in. Several cannibals stood around with spears poised, lest I somehow conjure my way out of my bonds.

I spent several painful, tedious hours thus. At dawn, I was picked up again, carried to the largest tent, and dumped inside before the high command.

This was my first chance to see Paaluans closely in good light. They were a tall folk, mostly lean, albeit there were a few stout ones among them. They had black—or at least very dark brown—skins. Their heads were covered by curly mops of black or brown hair, and they wore beards as well.

Unlike the Novarians and the Shvenites, they had no tabu against public nudity. Save for some who wore pieces of leather armor, and the feather cloaks of the high officers, they went completely naked. Their dark skins were painted with gaudy designs of several colors, red and white being the favorites. Far from concealing their sexual organs, as do most Prime Planers, they painted them in contrasting colors to make them more conspicuous.

They had low foreheads and large bony ridges above their eyes, on which the brows grew, so that their dark eyes seemed to peer out from little caverns. Their noses were extremely wide and flat, with no bridge. The mouths that opened in those great curly beards were very wide.

On a drum in the midst of the tent, surrounded by lesser officers and guards, sat the central figure in this tableau. He had a luxuriant, curly beard, turning from black to gray. Around his neck hung a golden chain, whence depended, below his beard, a large golden plaque or medallion—perhaps his insigne of rank.

Among the attendants was one who looked like a Novarian. He wore Novarian costume, but over it a leathern cuirass of Paaluan pattern.

There was talk, in an unfamiliar language, among these men. They stared at me as they spoke. At last the Novarian said:

"What are you, creature? Can you speak a human tongue?"

Since I still had the rope around my jaws, I could only grunt. The men presently saw my difficulty. With a laugh, one cut the jaw rope.

"Thank you, sir," I said.

"Oh," said the Novarian, "you speak Novarian?"

"Aye, sir. Whom have I the pleasure of addressing?"

"Charondas of Xylar, chief engineering officer to His Excellency General Ulola, commander of this foraging expedition."

"Sir," I said, "is it not unusual for a Novarian to occupy such a position in this foreign army?"

"Very," said Charondas. "I am now, however, an honorary Paaluan, having changed my allegiance. One must dwell amongst the Paaluans to appreciate their virtues; they are true gentlemen."

"And the gentleman on the drum, I take it, is General Ulola?"

"Aye."

"Well, kindly convey my respects to him, since I speak not his language."

Charondas translated, and the Paaluans burst into laughter. The renegade explained: "They're amused that a prisoner—and an inhuman one at that—should, whilst lying bound by twenty pounds of rope, natheless display such courtly manners."

"They are the manners I was taught on my own plane," I said. "Now, could you please tell me—"

"Look here, creature," said Charondas, "it is for us to question, not you. First, who and what are you?"

I explained. The general spoke, and Charondas asked: "He would know if you are that same ouph who passed through our camp in the other direction, six or seven sennights ago?"

"I suppose I am. I know of no other Twelfth Planer hereabouts."

"This relieves the general's mind; he's been concerned lest the sentry who bore the tale had been suffering hallucinations. And now, what's your purpose in seeking stealthily to mich back into doomed Ir?"

"I am sorry, sir, but I do not think it proper to answer that question."

"We have ways of making prisoners talk," said Charondas.

Just then, an officer came in and handed the general the two copies of the proposed contract between the Irians and the Hruntings, which I had been carrying. After more converse, Ulola gave the documents to Charondas. The renegade unrolled one and began to read it aloud, translating into Paaluan.

When he had finished, there was more talk. Then Charondas said:

"Since these documents tell us what we need to know about your mission, we shan't have to question you. It but remains to decide what to do with you."

He spoke with the general and again to me: "It is

decided to execute you, as we do all Novarians we catch. The general says, however, that we shall not eat you, for you might disagree with us. You'll be served to our dragons instead."

"Well, sirs," I said, "you have me in a position to do as you please with me. But if you will pardon my saying so, such an act does seem a bit drastic, when I have only striven to furnish satisfaction and obey my masters' hest."

Charondas translated this remark and the general's reply. The ensuing indirect discussion between me and the general went as follows: "Demon, we have nought against your kind as a whole. But, by working for the Novarians, you have incurred their guilt. You have committed a moral outrage that merits instant death."

"How so, General?"

"The Novarians, like the other folk of this continent, are irredeemably wicked and therefore should be destroyed."

"What does their wickedness consist of, sir?"

"In making war upon one another. We have looked into the matter and know they are all given to this vile practice."

"But, General, you are currently making war upon them, are you not? Wherein, then, lies your right to judge them?"

"Oh, we are not making war! We are conducting a foraging or harvesting expedition. We harvest a crop—a human crop—and we do it for the simple, normal, wholesome purpose of feeding our people. Since all creatures must eat, this is a natural and hence moral procedure. But to slay men for no good reason is wicked and immoral. Those who practice it deserve no mercy."

"But, General, I am told that the folk of this continent, when they make war, claim to have equally just reasons."

"What reasons? So that some political adventurer can extend his rule over more human beings, or seize their wealth, or convert them to his particular superstition, or kill them off so that his own folk can occupy their land?"

"How about those who defend themselves against such attacks? We demons of my plane do not practice war, but we do recognize the right of self-defense."

"That is a mere pretext. Two of these nations go to war, each claiming the other has attacked it, which is obviously absurd—albeit the most diligent inquiry might not be able to assign the true blame. Besides, if one of these paleface nations defends itself now, you can be sure that it has attacked some neighbor in the past.

"Nay, the only legitimate reason for slaying another human being is to eat him. So the only sensible thing is to round up the whole fractious lot, salt them down, and consume them. Since we Paaluans do not engage in war, we are obviously more moral than the palefaces, and it is therefore right and proper that we should so use them.

"But enough of this, demon. We have sentenced you to death, which is normally by decapitation. Charondas tells me, however, that you demons are of very tough fiber, and an ordinary ax or sword might give you no more than a flesh wound. Have you any suggestions?"

"Yes, General. Commute my sentence to banishment back to my own plane."

"Ha ha, very funny." Ulola spoke to Charondas, who replied in Paaluan. Then Charondas said to me:

"The general has commissioned me to build a beheading machine that shall take care of you, demon. A few hours should suffice. We shall see you anon."

Several soldiers bore me back to the inclosure, dumped me in, and stood guard over me. The day was one of the most unpleasant of my Prime Plane experience, combining apprehension with tedium. None fetched me water or did aught else to alleviate my discomfort. I had no hope of rescue by the Hruntings, since Hvaednir had decided not to move until I brought the signed contract back from Ir.

Under the circumstances, there was nothing else for me to do but sink into a digestive torpor. I was getting muckle tired of being mewed up in this tyrannous manner.

Early next day, I was dragged out of the inclosure and taken to a place before the general's tent. A gang of Paaluans were putting the finishing touches on Charondas' machine. This consisted of, first, a beheading block of the conventional kind, grooved for the reception of the victim's neck and chin. Fifteen feet away stood a massive wooden framework, in which a log was pivoted at one end. The lower end of this pole was fitted with a short axle, which in turn revolved in a pair of stout uprights. The upper end bore a huge blade, like an ax blade but several times as large. The Paaluan smiths must have worked all day and all night to get this piece of steel ready.

Beyond the pole and its foundation, a tall, three-legged wooden structure provided support for a pulley, over which ran the rope that held the log nearly upright. When the rope was released, the log would fall forward, bringing the blade down on the block—probably with enough force to split it in twain. This engine would have done for beheading a mammoth.

As the Paaluans hauled me to the block and laid my neck across it, I called out to General Ulola, who stood nearby with his officers:

"Sir, permit me to say that I truly believe this to be an unjustifiable and imprudent procedure. Yesterday I lacked the time to marshal my arguments in logical order, but if you will defer this function until I can explain, I am sure I can convince you—"

General Ulola said something to Charondas, who laughed and said to me: "O Zdim, the general wonders at a being who, about to lose his head, can still argue quillets of logic."

Charondas spoke to another Paaluan, who stepped to the tall tripod of timber with an ax. I saw that he meant to sever the rope that held the pole against falling. Ulola raised his arm to signal the ax man.

Before the general could lower his arm, there came a trumpet blast. This was followed by more trumpet calls, whistles, drums, and general uproar. Paaluans ran hither and thither, shouting. Some went by, pulling on their armor. The general, too, ran off. Dragon-lizards waddled past me with armed men on their backs.

Bound as I was, I could not truly see what was happening. From the noise, I inferred that Hvaednir must have changed his mind and attacked the camp.

The noise waxed even louder. I could discern the clatter of weapons and the screams of wounded men. After some time, the racket receded, as if the battle were rolling away from the camp. Had Hvaednir been repulsed?

Then the noise rose again, but from another direction. A few Paaluans ran past. After them came a multitude in the garb of Novarian sailors. They swirled past and out of sight.

A few lingered. One, in an officer's uniform, said: "And what in the nine hells is this?"

"Sir," I said, "permit me. I am a demon named Zdim, in the service of the Syndicate of Ir. To whom have I the pleasure of speaking?"

"Well, what do you here? Oh, I see; the cannibals were about to shorten you by a head. Ho, Zarko! Cut not that rope! Come hither and sever this thing's bonds. If it be a foe of the cannibals, it must be a friend of ours."

The sailor cut the ropes that bound me. While rubbing my limbs to restore circulation, I again asked the name of my rescuer.

"I am Diodis, High Admiral of Zolon," said the officer. I knew that the High Admiral was the chief executive of that island principality. "Explanations were too long for now, and I must forth with my men."

"Sir," said I, "if you will kindly lend me a weapon, I shall be glad to play my part in this affray, since the Paaluans have given me no cause to love them."

"Better not mix it in the front ranks, lest you be slain in ignorance by one of your own side. I have it! You shall stay by me as a bodyguard, eh? Come along!" he barked, and trotted off towards the main gate.

I followed the admiral, who had a brusquely authoritative way not easy to gainsay. We climbed a watchtower that flanked the main gate, whence we had a splendid view. A stream of messengers came and went, swarming up and down the ladder to our eyrie.

Before us, an extraordinary sight was spread out. To avoid confusion, permit me to summarize what I learnt later, piece by piece, about the situation.

Having destroyed the pirates of Algarth, the Zolonian fleet had sailed back to Chemnis to collect their pay from the Syndicate before returning to Zolon. Arriving at Chemnis, however, they found the harbor full of strange-looking craft manned by small numbers of naked black men, who shot arrows at them as they neared. The admiral ordered an attack and soon captured all the strange ships.

The admiral deduced that the main Paaluan force had marched up the Kyamos to attack Ir. So he chose a fleet of vessels of shallow draft, both Zolonian and Paaluan. He loaded them with armed men and brought them up the Kyamos. They anchored at the mouth of the unnavigable Vomantikon and marched up that affluent.

The Hrunting scouts saw this force, and the chiefs sent to demand their purpose. When the nomads learnt that the Zolonians meant to break the siege of Ir, they decided that, if they expected any pay at all for their long march, they needs must attack the Paaluans themselves, before the Zolonians could do so. Although the Zolonian force was small compared to their own, there was a chance that a surprise attack would rout the cannibals. Then the Irians would refuse to pay the Hrunting army one penny, on the ground that they had done nought to earn it.

The Hrunting chiefs were not rash. The five hundred Irians, who had arrived in the camp, were sent out as a decoy force, with a few hundred Hrunting horsemen to protect them from being surrounded. The Irians attacked the camp but let themselves be driven back. Filled with ardor, the Paaluan army poured out of the camp in pursuit—dragons, bouncers, and foot.

As soon as the Paaluans were clear of the camp, Yurog cast his cold spell. Down from the sky roared freezing winds. These not only discomfited the naked cannibals but also slowed the dragons to a gradual stop, like some mechanism that has run down. Now they stood like so many gray stone statues all over the plain, some with one leg lifted for the next step.

Then over the ridge separating the two camps came the rest of the Hrunting army, with its great block of mammoths in the middle. The cold was nothing to the Shvenites in their furs and sheepskins and to the mammoths in their hairy hides.

Meanwhile, the Zolonians entered the nearly vacant Paaluan camp, sweeping the few cannibals there before them. The sailors passed on out the front gate to assail the Paaluans in the rear.

But the cannibals, for all their strange customs, were fell fighters. Their dragons might be immobilized, their bouncer cavalry be scattered like chaff, their bodies be littering the plain, and they be surrounded and outnumbered. Natheless, the survivors formed a vast hollow square, with pikes bristling on all sides, and stood fast.

From within the square, their archers sent flight after flight of high-arching arrows, and their javelineers cast twirl-spears. They beat off charge after charge by foot, horse, and mammoth. Each attack left more bodies piled in front of the steady ranks of the spearmen. The Hrunting horse archers whirled past the square, pouring shafts into the massed ranks. When a Paaluan fell, his comrades closed the gap.

I was surprised that the first charge of mammoths did not roll over the cannibals and scatter them, but then I saw what they did. As the hairy monsters shuffled forward, with leathern sleeves on their trunks to protect them from sword cuts, the Paaluan wizards sent illusions of flying monsters against them. Squealing with terror and shaking their heads, the mammoths turned back.

Beside me in the tower, Admiral Diodis cursed and prayed, while messengers came and went. His speech was disjointed:

"Tell Captain Furio to move men from his left wing to his right!—Zevatas, king of the gods, help thy faithful worshipers—by Vaisus' brazen arse, get *in* there! Get close, so they can't use their pikes!—Franda, mother of gods—Tell Lieutenant Omphes he hangs back; if he bestir himself not, he'll hang *up* later . . ."

Then another force arrived. This was an army of gaunt, pallid men from the city of Ir. They jog-trotted through the Paaluan camp, past our tower, and out on the battlefield. Their trumpets warned the Zolonians to clear the path, and they went through the gap at a run.

The Irians crashed into the hollow square with a fury that nought could withstand. Men climbed over the bodies of their fellows to get at their foes. When their spears were broken, they fought with their swords; when they lost their swords, with their daggers; when these had gone, with nails and teeth. In a trice they had broken the square and were pouring into the interior, spearing and swording Paaluans in the back.

At the same time, another charge by the mammoths got home. The wizards inside the square were too busy being slain to cast another spell. The beasts plowed into the foe, swinging their heads. With each jerk, one or two cannibals would be caught by the huge tusks and sent flying.

The dust became so thick that it was hard to see anything. Little by little, Paaluan fugitives appeared out of the cloud, racing across the plain and throwing away weapons and armor. After them came Hvaednir's horsemen, shooting and spearing.

Of the original seven thousand Paaluans who had marched up the Kyamos, a little over six thousand were left at the beginning of the battle, the rest having perished in the siege or succumbed to sickness. Of this six thousand-odd, the great majority fell on the field, for no prisoners were taken. A few got away; but, lacking means to cross the Western Ocean, all were hunted down and slain during the ensuing months.

The greater part of the Paaluan losses took place after the Irians pierced the square and the formation began to break up. By contrast, of the nearly ten thousand men that fought against the cannibals that day, several hundred were killed or later died of their wounds. This was a sizable loss, but still only a small fraction of that of their foes. Such disparity in losses is not, I am told, unusual in battles on the Prime Plane, since a crowd of fleeing men can be slaughtered with comparative ease and safety by their pursuers.

Strictly speaking, one prisoner was taken: General Ulola, who was found wounded on the field. A quick-witted Irian officer stopped the soldiers from killing him as they were doing with other wounded cannibals. Rather than slay him at once, the Irians took the rest of the day to try and formally condemn him.

General Segovian acted as chief justicer. Since Charondas the renegade had prudently disappeared, there was nobody to translate for the general. He made some vehement but unintelligible speeches. My tendrils told me that he was filled with righteous indignation, that he should be punished for doing what he considered only right and proper.

In any case, he was found guilty and, despite his struggles and vociferous protests, placed on the heads-man's block prepared for me. An Irian cut the rope. Down came the log, *crash*, and off flew General Ulola's head.

I was sorry in a way. If he had been spared and I could have learnt to communicate with him, there were some interesting philosophical points on the morality of cannibalism, which he had brought up, which I should have been glad to pursue further. After all, I had eaten Prime Planers myself, even if I had never wantonly hunted them for aliment. But then, human beings have no due appreciation of abstract questions.

The battle had another curious consequence. The dragons had been frozen stiff by Yurog's spell, but the spell did not last for ay. Our victorious fighters had all but forgotten the statuesque reptiles when they began to thaw out and move. The commanders at once ordered their men to slay the monsters. This they did to a number; but not a few, no longer under control of their Paaluan masters, fled the battlefield and escaped. Some were hunted down. But I later heard rumors of dragon-lizards dwelling in the great Marsh of Moru, in southern Xylar, where the clime may be mild enough to sustain them the year around.

XI

PRINCE HVAEDNIR

I HAVE read many of those imaginary narratives that Prime Planers compose for one another's amusement, which are called "fiction." We have nothing like this on the Twelfth Plane, being too logical and literal-minded a species to enjoy it. I confess, however, that I have acquired a taste for the stuff, even though my fellow demons look at me askance as if I had become addicted to a dangerous narcotic.

In these imaginary narratives, called "stories," the human authors assume that the climax of a story solves all the problems posed and brings the action to a neat, tidy end. In a story, the battle of Ir would have been the climax. Then the hero would have mated with the heroine, the villains would have been destroyed, and the leading survivors, it is implied, would have lived happily ever after.

In real life, it is different. After this battle, the survivors continued their lives as before, with the usual ups and downs of fortune. Sometimes they profited from their virtues or suffered from their faults; sometimes the inscrutable workings of fate raised them high or cast them low irrespective of their merits.

Prince Hvaednir was overseeing the care of his wounded after the battle and the merciful cutting of the throats of those who seemed likely to die. General Segovian approached him and spoke, but neither could understand the other. Hvaednir looked around for Shnorri. Not finding him, he sighted me, standing with Admiral Diodis. The admiral was engaged in similar duties. Hvaednir called:

"Ho, Zdim! Come hither and interpret."

"With your kind permission, Admiral," I said. "Prince Hvaednir wants me."

"Is that the Hruntings' commander?" said the admiral. "I'll have a word with him myself."

Presently I was making formal introductions among the three commanders and translating for them. When amenities had been exchanged, Hvaednir asked:

"Can I do aught for you, General?"

"Food," said Segovian. "The Irians starve."

"You shall have it. Admiral, what can we do about this?"

"We have spare food in the ships. How about you?"

"We can match you for the supplies in our camp. But after today, I know not . . ."

"Permit me, Prince," said the admiral. "Your force is full of daredevil riders. Why not send messengers north, east, and south, with word of this victory? Whilst they're at it, they can let it be known that any farmer or produce merchant who wishes a quick profit has but to get a cartload of edibles to Ir ahead of the rush."

Hvaednir made a mow. "Appealing to base commercial lusts is not the way *we* do things, but I suppose you know your Novarians."

The admiral chuckled. " 'Base commercial lusts' forsooth! Sink me if you don't see that they bring results."

Indeed they did. On the second day after the battle, laden asses and creaking farm carts began to arrive from Solymbria, Metouro, and Xylar. How they covered such distances in that time I know not. Some must have driven their beasts all night.

Meanwhile, Hvaednir and the admiral agreed to distribute enough food from their stores to furnish every Irian in the city one good repast. General Segovian said:

"Prince, why come you not into the city ere nightfall, to receive the plaudits of a grateful people?"

Hvaednir glanced down at his armor, covered with dust and blood. "What, looking like this? I mean, my dear sir, I am too fatigued tonight. Tomorrow I shall be glad to. The food, however, shall go forthwith."

I bid the admiral farewell and accompanied Prince

Hvaednir back to the camp. Shnorri, having received a minor wound in the arm, was there ahead of us. Hvaednir clapped his cousin on the back, bringing a yell of pain from the wounded man.

"A murrain!" said Shnorri. "Now you have started this thing to bleeding again."

"I am sorry," said Hvaednir. "I never thought . . . But it was a fine battle, was it not?"

"If we do not have to fight the Gendings within a year, what of our losses," said Shnorri.

"Oh, you are always glooming. Wine! Where in the afterworld are those worthless servants of ours? Ah, there you are! Wine, and speedily!" When the flagon and bottle were brought, he drank deep. "You know, cousin, I like this southern land. Think of being able to drink real wine the year round—none of our weak, sour steppe beer!"

"Novaria in summer is too cursed hot for me," said Shnorri, sweating.

Hvaednir had food for the three of us brought to the tent, but he kept on drinking at a rate that promised trouble. Sure enough, the sun had been down scarce an hour when the golden prince began to utter thoughts that a prudent being would have kept to himself.

"Why in the nine hells," he growled, "should I have to wait around forever for old winter-locks to die, when I could carve out a country of my own? For a beginning, a few hundred stout warriors were enough to seize Ir from these craven money-grubbers—"

"I notice that Segovian's men were no cravens in to-day's affray," said Shnorri.

"Oh, that! I daresay I could beat some proper no-madic discipline into them. Might even make warriors of them. And why not? Am I not the victor of the greatest battle of our time? The bards will sing of it. By Greipnek's beard once given a good start, I shall be a greater conqueror than Heilsung the Invincible . . ."

Shnorri said: "Zdim, you had better go to your own tent. I shall see you at daybreak."

Evidently, Shnorri did not wish me to overhear any more of his cousin's indiscretions. I bade them good night and returned to my quarters, where I sat in thought. It occurred to me that I ought to slip away from the camp under cover of darkness, go to Ir, and warn the Syndicate against Hvaednir's burgeoning ambitions.

When I had come to this conclusion, I discovered that a sentry had been posted at my tent. This did not utterly dismay me, because I foresaw that in the letdown after the battle, discipline would relax. In the normal course of events, the sentry would probably get drunk himself, wander off, or fall asleep. I had only to watch and wait for an hour or two ...

The next thing I knew, the dawn sun was streaming in through the flap of my tent and Shnorri was shaking me awake. "Up, lazybones!" he cried. "We are about to set out in the grand procession to Ir, to receive the plaudits of a grateful people. You must come with us as interpreter for Hvaednir; I shall have too many other duties."

I shook myself awake. I had slept right through the time when I meant to go to Ir to warn the Irians. Although this was a grave lapse on my part, I had some excuse, having had no proper sleep for two days and nights. I asked Shnorri, who still had one arm in a sling:

"Prince, what about that plan I heard Hvaednir broach last night, of seizing Ir and using it as a base for further empery?"

"Pooh! That was just your sweet Novarian wine talking. I argued him out of such folly. He has solemnly promised me that, if Ir keep faith with him, he will do the same by Ir."

"He seemed like a mild enough youth back in Shven. What has gotten into him?"

"Methinks yesterday's victory has gone to his head—that, and having his own first independent command. On the steppe, the cham kept him on a tight rein. But I am sure he will be all right."

"Too bad you are not next in line. You are much wiser than he."

"Hush, demon! Such thoughts were treasonable, albeit I thank you for the compliment. Hvaednir is not really stupid—merely spoiled and of commonplace mind—and he is far handsomer than I. This counts among Shvenites. Moreover, he is a better man of his hands than I shall ever be; I am too fat for leading charges. But enough of this haver. Don some garment and come with us."

We marched across the battlefield, through the Paaluans' camp—already partly dismantled—and to Ardyman's Tower. We climbed the broad spiral ramp and entered the main portal, now open for the first time in over two months. Inside, the courtyard resounded with the clatter of workmen repairing the great mirror, which had been damaged but never quite put out of operation by the besiegers' catapult missiles.

The entire Syndicate, which now included Her Excellency Roska sar-Blixens, met us. Chief Syndic Jimmon—a little thinner but still comfortably upholstered—made a speech. He read a citation from a parchment scroll and handed Hvaednir a symbolic key to the city. These formalities accomplished, Jimmon said to me:

"Hail, O Zdim! You'll have some fascinating tales to tell us when the ceremonies are over, eh? Now, Prince, we have laid out a suitable parade route. We shall march the length of Ardyman Avenue, then turn right . . ."

We marched into the underground city, where the only illumination was furnished by beams of sunlight reflected from mirror to mirror. In front, to the beat of drums, marched a company of Hruntings, armed to the teeth; then Shnorri with a couple of chiefs and several Syndics; then more warriors. Then came Hvaednir, Jimmon, and the rest of the chiefs; then Admiral Diodis and some of his sailors, and so forth. Jimmon walked on one side of Hvaednir and I on the other. Hvaednir had garbed himself in the most awesome costume that the Hruntings' wardrobe afforded. He wore a winged golden helm, a fur-edged white woollen tunic embroidered in gold thread, and a jeweled sword. He could have been one of the Prime Plane's gods.

Having enjoyed their first good meal since the beginning of the siege, the Irians cheered us mightily. In that confined space, the reverberating sound hurt the ears. I watched for a chance to slip away and warn the Syndics against Hvaednir, but none came.

The parade ended at the Guildhall, which was filled with officers of the guilds and most of the merchant class. For three hours I listened to speeches and translated Novarian to Shvenish and vice versa. Jimmon made the longest one; Hvaednir, the shortest. All speeches were trains of well-worn stock phrases: "Deadly perils . . . gallant allies . . . bloodthirsty savages . . . immortal fatherland . . . doughty warriors . . . hour of need . . . noble ancestors . . . intrepid heroes . . . implacable foes . . . eternal friendship . . . undying gratitude . . ." and so on.

The audience stood and applauded when all was done. Then the Syndics, Admiral Diodis, General Segovian, Hvaednir, Shnorri, and I went to dinner in one of the smaller chambers. So many pressed compliments upon Hvaednir that I was almost kept too busy translating to eat.

Hvaednir ate and drank heartily; especially, he drank. At first he displayed the roynish table manners of the steppe, but as Shnorri kept nudging him in the ribs, he began to imitate Novarian customs.

When it was over, Hvaednir cleared his throat and stood up, saying: "Your Excellencies! On behalf of my cousin, Prince Shnorri, and myself, I—ah—I extend heartfelt thanks for this entertainment and for the many honors bestowed upon us this morning.

"Now, however, we must come to practical matters. Your envoy, the worthy Zdim, overcame deadly perils to reach the headquarters of the Hruntings and importune us to send this expeditionary force. Zdim started out with a written offer of compensation but lost his papers to the cave-men of the Ellornas. He remembered the terms, however, and, after the usual bargaining, an oral understanding was reached.

"When we reached the Kyamos, we dispatched Zdim to gain entrance to the city, confirm this understanding in writing, and return to us with your signatures.

Again, misfortune robbed him of the documents, and he came close to losing his life as well.

"All is not lost, however." Hvaednir produced from his embroidered jacket the two copies, somewhat tattered, of the agreement that we had drawn up in the camp the night before the battle. "These were picked up in the cannibals' camp. I am sure that, in recognition of the services of the fearless Hrunting warriors in saving your city, there will be no difficulty about getting you to append your signatures now and to begin payment forthwith."

The smile that usually pervaded Jimmon's round face was wiped off. "Humph. Of course, noble sir, none would dream of withholding a just reward from our heroic feodaries. But may I have the actual terms agreed upon, pray?"

Hvaednir passed one of the two copies to Jimmon. The other he handed to Shnorri, saying: "Read this aloud, cousin, since you speak the language and read with more facility than I."

When Shnorri had finished, Jimmon arose, dangling his reading glass by its ribbon. He launched into another verbose encomium on the valor of the Hruntings.

"But," he continued, "we must, of course, take certain realities into account. The city has suffered dreadfully during this cruel siege, and our resources will be sorely strained during the recovery. It is also a fact that, for all their dash and heroism, the Hruntings were not the only ones to take part in the battle. Admiral Diodis' gallant tars played their role, to say nought of our own Irians.

"And furthermore, noble Prince, it is also a fact that no true legal obligation exists on our part, since the gage in question was not signed before the fact. Of course, with generosity and goodwill on all sides, I am sure that an amicable settlement can be reached amongst us . . ."

Gods of Ning, I thought, is the fool going to try to wriggle out of paying the nomad, when the latter has him in his power?

". . . and so, dear friend and noble colleague, I am

sure you will agree to the necessity of—ah—adjusting these demands in accordance with realities."

"What had you in mind?" said Hvaednir in a tight voice.

"Oh, something on the order of twopence a man a day, with nought extra for the mammoths. The beasts have after all been eating our fine Irian hay to their hearts' content—"

Prince Hvaednir's face turned crimson. "Horse dung!" he roared. "Last night I promised that, if Ir kept faith with me, I would do likewise; but if not, then not. No brave steppe warrior permits some paper law to stop him from doing right. You welshers are condemned from your own mouths, and be what follows on your own heads!"

He blew a blast on a silver whistle. A score of Hruntings filed into the chamber with bared swords and took positions behind the other diners. Roska screamed.

"One false move, and off go your heads," said Hvaednir. "I hereby pronounce myself king of Ir and of such other lands as may in the future come under my sway. Chief Fikken!"

"Aye, my lord?"

"Pass the word to my chiefs to carry out the plan I laid out for them last night. First, I wish every bit of gold, silver, and jewels in Ir taken from wherever it now is and brought to the Guildhall. I proclaim all such valuables part of my royal treasury. We shall begin by searching those present—ho, where is the admiral?"

There was a general turning of heads, until a Syndic said: "He excused himself, saying he had to visit the jakes."

"Find him!" said Hvaednir. A couple of Hruntings were dispatched on this mission, but without success. Sensing what was coming, the admiral had slipped out of Ir altogether.

The Syndics, bursting with indignation but not daring to complain, submitted to having their purses dumped out on the table. Hvaednir returned to each man the copper coins in his possession but swept the gold and silver into a heap.

"I—I'm sorry," said Roska, "but I left my purse at home."

"We will take care of that later," said Hvaednir cheerfully. "This is but a beginning, my dear subjects."

Shnorri, sweating freely, kept his mouth shut. Hvaednir directed us all to rise and to file back into the main hall, where we had listened to speeches that morning. From outside came the sound of many running feet and the outcries of Irians as their cave-homes were invaded and searched. Presently warriors began to enter the Guildhall, bowed under bulging sacks of coin and precious objects. They dumped the sacks on the floor, and Hvaednir put the Syndicate's clerks to sorting the loot and totting up its value.

Now and then a disturbance broke out as some Irians resisted the sack. There were shouts and the clang of arms. A couple of wounded Hruntings were brought in, while others reported that the rebels had been slain out of hand.

The Syndics sat in a glum row, guarded by Hruntings. They carried on fierce recriminations under their breaths: "I knew Jimmon's plan would bring disaster . . ." "Rubbish! You were as keen for it as any last night . . ."

Shnorri, who had been talking to some of the chiefs, approached Hvaednir and said: "Cousin, what plan you with our army? You could not settle them all here even if they were willing, and most of them wish to return to Shven forthwith. Summer wanes, and snow will close the Needle's Eye by the Month of the Bear."

"I will call for volunteers to remain," said Hvaednir. "The rest may go home when they list. You, Shnorri, shall lead them. For all I care, you may take my place as heir apparent to Theorik. I shall have my hands full here."

Shnorri sighed. "I suppose I must. I wish now that, when I was offered a post on the faculty of the Academy of Othomae, I had taken it."

Hvaednir spent a couple of hours in organizing his rule and appointing cronies to posts. Then he gave a prodigious yawn.

"Madam Roska," he said, "you left your purse at home, I believe. May I impose upon your hospitality?"

"Of a surety, Your Majesty."

"Then lead us thither. You, too, Zdim, lest I be unable to converse with this beautiful lady."

We set out for Roska's house, preceded and followed by bodyguards. Almost at the front door of the house, a groan attracted our attention. A wounded Hrunting lay in the shadow at the side of the street.

Hvacdnir commanded that the bodyguards carry the man into Roska's house. Inside, the man was laid on a sofa. As Hvaednir was examining him, he expired.

"He must have been stabbed by some Irian who was not fain to give up his gold," said Hvaednir. "We cannot brook this, but I see not how to find the culprit." He looked puzzled, then said to a guard: "Go, fetch my cousin, Prince Shnorri. I must ask his rede."

The other guards he posted before the house. Roska's servants peeked timidly out through door cracks. Hvaednir lowered his huge form into a chair, doffed his golden helmet and jeweled baldric, and rubbed his forehead.

"By Greipnek's nose, I am fordone!" he said. "I think I will move the capital of the kingdom to some more normal city. Being cooped up in this glorified cavern gives me the shudders."

"Now, about my purse . . ." began Roska, but Hvaednir held up a hand.

"I would not think of raping so gracious a lady of her gold. You may keep your pelf. But may I beg a stoup of wine?"

"Awad!" she called.

The swarthy Fediruni shuffled timidly into the room. When he saw me, he grinned through his pointed black beard. Roska sent him for wine, which Hvaednir was soon drinking in great gulps.

"I need a friend amongst the Irians," he said abruptly. "I know how many would resent today's events, even though they brought them upon themselves. In time, I hope to show that a king of the noble Hruntings will rule them far more justly than those lucre-loving Syndics."

He gulped down another goblet, then stood up unsteadily. "Roska, my dear, would you care to show me your house?"

"Why, certes, Your Majesty."

"Let us, then. Remain here, Zdim. I needs must practice my few phrases of Novarian on our gracious hostess. If I am to rule them, it behooves me to learn their clack."

Roska took Hvaednir on a brief tour of the living room, pointing out the pictures, vases, and other ornaments. Then they departed up the stairs.

Awad scuttled in and squeezed my hands. "Master Zdim! It is good to see you. The mistress followed your adventures in her scry stone and told us of some of them, but we would hear the story from your own mouth. You'll be returning to service here, I hope?"

"I know not, yet," I said. "I could use a little more of that wine, myself. This is from Vindium, is it not?"

"Aye. And now for the story. You left on the first day of the Month of the Eagle—"

A scream from upstairs interrupted. Since my primary duty was still to Madam Roska, I leaped from the chair and bounded up the stairs, followed by Awad.

Another scream was followed by Roska's cry of "Zdim! Save me!"

The sound came from her bedchamber. Thither I rushed. In the chamber were Roska and Hvaednir. Roska, with her gown torn from her body, lay supine on the bed. Hvaednir stooped over her with one knee on the bed. The prince was trying to hold down Roska with one hand while he fumbled with the fastening of his breeks with the other.

I had read of this Prime Plane practice called "rape," in which a male human being copulates with a female against her will. We have nothing like that on the Twelfth Plane, and I had wondered how certain mechanical problems in carrying out this operation—deemed a crime among most human societies—were surmounted.

Having been commanded by Roska to save her, however, I could not indulge my curiosity by standing back and watching with philosophical objectivity. I leaped to the task without stopping to think out all its logical implications. I sprang upon Hvaednir from behind, fastened my talons in his torso, and pulled him back from the bed.

The man fought free of my grasp, although his tunic and the skin beneath it were badly torn in the process. He fetched me a buffet beneath the jaw that staggered me and would, I daresay, have sent a Prime Planer clear across the room. Then we grappled again. I tried to fang his throat, but he got an elbow under my jaw and held me away.

I was amazed at the man's strength. I had engaged in hand-to-hand combat with Prime Planers before and found them all comparative weaklings. Not only, however, was Hvaednir a virtual giant among Novarians— taller than I and much heavier—but also his muscles seemed to be of unusually good quality. His physical strength was little if any below my own.

We staggered about, stamping, tearing, and kicking. Neither seemed able to gain a definitive advantage. Then I felt a knife hilt pressed into my hand. I drove the blade into Hvaednir's side, once, twice, and thrice.

The huge Hrunting groaned and jerked in my grasp, and the strength fled swiftly from his frame. As I released him, he slumped to the floor. Behind him, little Awad pointed to the long, curved dagger in my hand.

"Mine," he said.

"I thank you," I said, bending over my fallen antagonist.

A quick examination disclosed that Hvaednir, the would-be king of Ir, was dead. Madam Roska sat up on the bed, pulling a sheet about her nakedness. She said:

"Good gods, Zdim! Why slew you him?"

"What? Why, madam, I heard your cry for help and endeavored to obey your commands. Did you not wish it?"

"Nay! I could not permit him to have his will of me without a ladylike show of resistance, but this! It may cost us all our lives."

"I am sorry, madam, but nobody had explained these quiddities to me. I try to give satisfaction."

"I suppose you do, poor dear Zdim. But my so-called virtue is not a matter of such great moment as all that, since I am a widow old enough to be this barbarian's mother. I might even have enjoyed it after he got under way. Later, as his mistress, I might have guided him for the good of Ir.

"Natheless, that's all by the bye. The pregnant question is: what now?"

I heard the voice of Shnorri, calling: "Cousin Hvaednir! Your Majesty! Where are you?"

"Shnorri is our only hope," I said. "Let me fetch him, pray." Without awaiting arguments, I put my head out the door and called: "Prince Shnorri! Up here! Come alone!"

"Is aught wrong?" said he as his head appeared at the top of the stairway.

"You shall judge, sir. Good or ill, it is of the utmost moment."

When he saw Hvaednir's body, he rushed over to it and confirmed that the man was dead. "Who did this? How befell it?"

"I will explain," I said, standing with my back to the door in case Shnorri attempted to rush out and summon his men. If needful, I should have slain him, told the bodyguards that their commanders were asleep, and fled the city. When I had finished, Shnorri said:

"I might have known the drunken fool would get into something like this. If only he had had a noble mind to go with that splendid body . . . But what now? The warriors will burn you over a slow fire if they find out. I understand your side of it; but the reason is that I have dwelt amongst Novarians and hence am only half nomad in outlook."

"Sir," I said, "marked you that corpse in the living room?"

"Aye, and I meant to ask about it."

I explained about the dead warrior. "Now," I said, "let us do as follows: tell the soldiers that the lady Roska retired to her room to rest; that the dead man, who was merely stunned and not gravely hurt, recovered consciousness, slipped upstairs, and essayed to rape Madam Roska; that Hvaednir, hearing her outcry, rushed to her rescue; and that in the affray, he and the warrior each dealt the other a mortal wound. Then there will be nobody to blame."

There was some argument over this plan, but none could think of a better. Roska slipped into the adjacent dressing room to make herself presentable. I told Shnorri:

"At least, if Ir be ruled by nomads, you were a better monarch than your late cousin."

"Not I!" quotha. "I shall be glad to get out of this beastly heat and to take the warriors with me, ere they be softened by Novarian luxury. Hvaednir's was a chancy scheme at best. A cleverer man might have carried it off; but then it would have weakened the horde back on the steppe. We shall need every man to confront the Gendings. Help me to carry the dead warrior up to this room, that our story shall hang together."

XII

ADMIRAL DIODIS

I SAID: "It strikes me, Prince Shnorri, that Madam Roska and I had better get out of Ir ere you announce your cousin's demise. You human beings are easily excited by rumors. If some of your men think up a story different from yours, I should not care to be in their power when it happened."

After some small debate, Shnorri acknowledged that we had right on our side. We went down to the living room, where Shnorri summoned a chief.

"Take these two outside Ardyman's Tower," he said, "and lend them horses from the general reserve herd."

A quarter-hour later, we were on our way. "Whither, O Zdim?" said Roska.

"Admiral Diodis, meseems, offers us the safest refuge till these things blow over. If attacked, he can sail down the Kyamos and away."

So it proved. The stout, grizzled admiral welcomed us heartily aboard his flagship. He had already recalled his men to the ships, and the shallow-draft fleet lay anchored well out from shore, so that surprise was unlikely.

Seated on Diodis' quarterdeck, we were served a hot, reddish-brown beverage. The admiral explained:

" 'Tis called 'tea' in its land of origin, which is Kuromon in the Far East. It comes in the form of dried leaves to Salimor, and thence to Janareth in the Inner Sea, and thence by land over the Lograms to Fedirun, and at last to the sea again at Iraz. Let's hope it will some day be for sale in Novaria, too. We need a good drink that won't make us drunk.

"Now, O Zdim, tell us the tale of your adventures."

I launched into my story. After I had been speaking for some minutes, however, I observed that Admiral Diodis and Madam Roska were paying me little heed. Instead, they were watching each other, betimes exchanging some irrelevant comment in an undertone. They smiled and laughed a lot.

At length, this became so marked that I let my narrative trail off while I enjoyed my tea. They never noticed.

The following day, Prince Shnorri and some of his chiefs rode to the water's edge and waved. The admiral and I were rowed in a longboat to within speaking distance.

"Come back to Ir and bid us farewell!" said Shnorri.

"Are you packed to depart?" asked the admiral.

"Certes. Fear not; there was no difficulty about the story of my cousin's death, and my own feelings are entirely friendly." Since he spoke Novarian, his chiefs could not understand him.

"We appreciate that," said Diodis, "but this will do as well as any place for a farewell."

"I know what you suspect, but it is not so. At noon

I shall light my cousin's funeral pyre and give the command to march. It were worth your while to be there, Admiral, since I understand that Ir owes you money, too. Now were the time to present your reckoning."

"But if you Shvenites have cleaned the city out—"

"We have not. I have taken only so much as was needed to meet Zdim's contract. The balance should suffice for Zolon's claims. Bring a guard of sailors if you trust us not. Or stay on your ships, if you prefer, and take your chances of collecting from the Syndicate later, when gratitude has been weakened by casuistry and self-interest."

"We'll come," said the admiral.

Prince Shnorri thrust a torch into the pyre, atop of which lay Hvaednir's body. As the roaring fire hid the corpse in flame and smoke, the ranked Hruntings burst into sobs. Hardly a cheek among them was not wet with tears. Shnorri said aside to me:

"Come back in a hundred years, Zdim, and you will find that Hvaednir has become the hero of a cycle of legends—the pure, noble, beautiful ideal of the Hruntings. His shortcomings will be forgotten, whilst his virtues will have been exaggerated out of all recognition."

We talked of this and that, and I said: "Pray tell me, Prince, you know Prime Planers better than I. See you that pair yonder, Admiral Diodis and Madam Roska?"

"Aye."

"Well, ever since we boarded the flagship yesterday, they have been acting out of character—at least, as far as I could judge their character—to so marked a degree that I am baffled, who thought myself fairly familiar with the oddities of Prime Plane nature."

"What puzzles you?"

"By herself, Roska sar-Blixens is a grave, reserved lady, a great dignity and presence, even if she be ever changing her mind. Admiral Diodis is gruff, positive, and forceful. Both are, one would say, as mature as one would ever expect of a human being. Yet, when together, they seem as full of careless laughter and foolish remarks as children, and they seem interested in each other to the exclusion of all else."

"It is simple," said Shnorri. "They are in love."

"Ah! I have read of this emotion in my studies, but never having witnessed the phenomenon I did not recognize it. Will they now mate?"

He shrugged. "How should I know? I know not if Diodis already have a wife; or, if he have, whether the laws of Zolon permit him to take a second. I daresay, however, that the old sea dog and your gracious mistress will presently find means to warm the same bed.

"And now we must part. If you ever get to Othomae, tell old Doctor Kylus that I wish I had taken his offer of a readership in the Academy. I know I am too fat, lazy, and good-natured to be a nomadic warrior chieftain, but the gods seem determined to make me one."

"Could you bear the Novarian summer heat? It seems to undo you."

"Yes, with a summer camp in the Lograms, even that."

"Then, what stops you from riding to Othomae and taking up this academic career?"

"Tribal duty and loyalty, curse them. Fare you well!"

With the help of two warriors, he heaved himself into the saddle. Then he waved to the crowd and trotted off. The squadrons of Hrunting horsemen swung into line behind him, and then went the mammoths and the rear guard. Shnorri might be a fine fellow, but we were all glad to see the last of that formidable host.

The dust of their departure had scarcely settled when the admiral, too, presented his scot for the expedition to Algarth and for his help against the Paaluans. Jimmon and the other Syndics looked aghast; but, thoroughly cowed, they did not dare to risk another clash. They paid. As they were counting out the money in the Guildhall under Diodis' watchful eye, Roska said:

"Everybody's being requited for his part in the rescue save the one man—I mean being—to whom we owe the most. That is my bondservant Zdim."

"By Thio's horns!" cried Jimmon. "We shall be beggared as it is, Roska. If you are fain to reward your demon, nought stops you."

She set her mouth in that expression that, among human beings, betokens stubbornness. " 'Twere only fair that, since all profited, all should share in the recompense. Am I not right, Diodis?"

"Sink me!" said the admiral. "It's no business of mine; but if you insist, my dear Roska, I must own that you are right as always. Perhaps, howsomever, it were well to ask Master Zdim what *he* would like. Don't assume that, like a mere human being, he lusts for silver and gold."

"Well, Zdim?" said Jimmon.

"Sirs," I said, "I seek to fulfill my obligations. But since you ask, what I should most like is to be freed from my indenture, like the other slaves and bondservants of Ir. Then I wish to be sent back to my own plane, to rejoin my wife and eggs. Oh, and besides, I should appreciate a few ingots of iron to be sent with me."

The relief on the Syndics' faces would have made me laugh, had I been capable of that human sound and had I possessed the human quality called a sense of humor.

The magical operation was performed in the sanctum of Doctor Maldivius, under the ruined temple of Psaan near Chemnis. Having by his magical arts avoided the cannibals' bouncer cavalry when they were scouring the land for human flesh, Maldivius had returned to his old abode. When I arrived, I was astonished to see another bent, white-haired figure.

"Yurog!" I cried. "What do you here? I thought you had returned to the Ellornas with the Hruntings."

"Me apprentice to Doctor Maldivius. Me learn to be great wizard."

To Maldivius I said: "Is it not unusual for a magician of advanced years to take as apprentice another as old as himself?"

"That's my business, demon," snapped Maldivius. "Yurog does what I tell him, which is more than I can say for the silly young bucks I've tried. Ahem. Now sit on those ingots in the pentacle."

Madam Roska stopped holding hands with the admiral long enough to step forward and plant a kiss on my muzzle. "Farewell, darling Zdim!" she said. "I've returned Maldivius' Sapphire to him to enlist his coöperation. Give my love to your wife and eggs."

"Thank you, madam. I have endeavored to give satisfaction."

Diodis added: "Do you demons need an admiral to organize your navy? I thought some day I should like to take a year off and see some other plane."

"Not practicing the art of war, we have no navies," I said. "But we do have shipping. If occasion arise, sir, I will tell the demons concerned of your interest."

I sat down on the two hundredweight ingots of iron. Maldivius and Yurog began their incantation. Ere the scene faded out, I waved to the several Prime Planers who had come to see me off. I was happy to have been able to keep in touch with these human beings to the end of my stay. Many others with whom I had come in contact, such as Bagardo the Great, Aithor of the Woods, and Gavindos the wrestler-archon, vanished from my ken; I know not what befell them.

I was glad to learn that Ungah the ape-man survived the cannibal war. A Paaluan sentry saw him in the camp and wounded him in the leg with a javelin. He would have been slain, but just then the uproar caused by my own discovery on the far side of the camp distracted the sentry, and Ungah escaped.

He got as far as the border of Metouro, but then his leg became so bad that he could no longer walk. He would have perished had not a local witch-wife taken him in and nursed him back to health. By the time he was able to travel on, the war was over; so he settled down with his rescuer to stay. I was told that she was a singularly ugly woman; but to Ungah she doubtless looked like a female of his own species and therefore just his heart's desire.

Provost Hwor looked at the two ingots. "Why the man did you not bring more with you?" he barked.

Expecting praise, I became wroth. "Because this is all their spell would carry across the dimensional barrier!" I cried. "If you like them not, send them back."

"There, there, my good Zdim, I meant no harm. Yeth will be delighted to see you half a year ahead of time."

"How fared our clutch of eggs?"

"Most of them hatched safely, I hear."

"Then I am off for home!"

A PETITION TO THE PROVOST OF NING, FROM ZDIM AKH'S SON AND HIS WIFE, YETH PTYG'S DAUGHTER:

You are familiar with the circumstances of my indenture on the Prime Plane a few years back. Having returned safely to the Twelfth Plane, I thought I should never again wish to see the Prime Plane, so vastly less rational, logical, and predictable than our own.

Now, however, that our offspring are of school age and hence independent, my wife and I should like to know if arrangements could be made for us to remove to the Prime Plane for an extended residence. In case the regulations require that an equal number of Prime Planers be moved to this plane to maintain the balance of energy, I know at least two Prime Planers who said they might like to shift to the Twelfth Plane. I will undertake to find them and arrange the transfer.

As for gaining my living, I have several plans in mind. For example, I have the name of a professor at one of their institutions of learning, who might have a position for me. After all, I am a trained philosopher and, from what I saw of the Prime Plane, I gather that amongst those folk the science of philosophy is in utter disarray. If that fail, I have other connections and acquaintances. Fear not that I shall be unable to earn an adequate income.

If you wonder why I present this request, know that, despite the hazards and hardships of life there and the rampant irrationality of its people, the world has many fascinations. One never gets bored, as I fear one often does in our well-run world. Something interesting is always happening.

Respectfully yours,
Zdim